I KEPT PRESSING THE

100-MILLION-YEAR BUTTON AND CAME OUT ON TOP

~THE UNBEATABLE REJECT SWORDSMAN~

4

T0247068

I brought my sword crashing down from above without hesitation.

"Grr..."

Idora crossed her lances and just barely blocked the attack. Our weapons locked, sending sparks flying. We both pushed, now engaged in a pure contest of strength.

"Haaa aaaaa aaa!"

Idora Luksmaria

A first year from White Lily Girls Academy, one of the Elite Five Academies. She is a prodigy known far and wide as the "Wonder Child." She has an intense duel with Allen in the Sword Master Festival.

"This is nothing. It's not too different from what I normally wear."

Rose Valencia

The legitimate heir of the Cherry Blossom Blade School of Swordcraft. She works as a waiter along with Lia for the cosplay café during the Thousand Blade Festival.

"Hmm-hmm. Did I surprise you?"

Lia Vesteria

A princess of Vesteria Kingdom who lives in the same room as Allen. She participates in the cosplay café during the Thousand Blade Festival.

"...Dodriel, give me your support."

"...Yes sir."

Dodriel Barton

Allen's bitter rival from Grand Swordcraft Academy. He joined the Black Organization after losing to Allen in a decisive duel.

Fuu Ludoras

One of the Black Organization's Thirteen Oracle Knights. He leads the Black Organization in an attack on Thousand Blade.

"You have my thanks, worms..."

A pitch-black darkness enveloped all of Thousand Blade Academy. Black stretched as far as the eye could see. Fuu slowly turned around and saw "Allen Rodol" standing uninjured and laughing maniacally.

Allen Rodol(?)

Another personality that resides within Allen. He possesses overwhelming strength, and his origins are unknown.

CONTENTS

I KEPT PRESSING THE 100-MILLION-YEAR BUTTON AND CAME OUT ON TOP

~THE UNBEATABLE REJECT SWORDSMAN~

4

SYUICHI TSUKISHIMA

Illustration by MOKYU

YEN ON

New York

I KEPT PRESSING THE 100-MILLION-YEAR BUTTON AND CAME OUT
ON TOP: ~THE UNBEATABLE REJECT SWORDSMAN~
SYUICHI TSUKISHIMA

Translation by Luke Hutton
Cover art by Mokyu

This book is a work of fiction. Names, characters, places, and incidents are the product
of the author's imagination or are used fictitiously. Any resemblance to actual events,
locales, or persons, living or dead, is coincidental.

I OKUNEN BUTTON O RENDA SHITA ORE HA, KIZUITARA SAIKYO NI
NATTE ITA Vol.4 ~RAKUDAI KENSHI NO GAKUIN MUSO~
©Syuichi Tsukishima, Mokyu 2020
First published in Japan in 2020 by KADOKAWA CORPORATION, Tokyo.
English translation rights arranged with KADOKAWA CORPORATION, Tokyo,
through TUTTLE-MORI AGENCY, INC., Tokyo

English translation © 2022 by Yen Press, LLC

Yen Press, LLC supports the right to free expression and the value of copyright.
The purpose of copyright is to encourage writers and artists to produce the creative
works that enrich our culture.

The scanning, uploading, and distribution of this book without permission is a theft
of the author's intellectual property. If you would like permission to use material from
the book (other than for review purposes), please contact the publisher. Thank you for
your support of the author's rights.

Yen On
150 West 30th Street, 19th Floor
New York, NY 10001

Visit us at yenpress.com
facebook.com/yenpress
twitter.com/yenpress
yenpress.tumblr.com
instagram.com/yenpress

First Yen On Edition: November 2022
Edited by Yen On Editorial: Leilah Labossiere
Designed by Yen Press Design: Andy Swist

Yen On is an imprint of Yen Press, LLC.
The Yen On name and logo are trademarks of Yen Press, LLC.

The publisher is not responsible for websites (or their content) that are not owned by
the publisher.

Library of Congress Cataloging-in-Publication Data
Names: Tsukishima, Syuichi, author. | Mokyu, illustrator. | Hutton, Luke, translator.
Title: I kept pressing the 100-million-year button and came out on top /
Syuichi Tsukishima ; illustration by Mokyu ; translation by Luke Hutton.
Other titles: Ichiokunen button o renda shita ore wa, kizuitara saikyo ni natte ita. English
Description: First Yen On edition. | New York, NY : Yen On, 2021–
Identifiers: LCCN 2021034588 | ISBN 9781975322342 (v. 1 ; trade paperback) |
ISBN 9781975322366 (v. 2 ; trade paperback) | ISBN 9781975322380
(v. 3 ; trade paperback) | ISBN 978-1975343163 (v. 4 ; trade paperback) |
Subjects: LCGFT: Fantasy fiction. | Light novels.
Classification: LCC PL876.S857 I3413 2021 | DDC 895.6/36—dc23
LC record available at https://lccn.loc.gov/2021034588

ISBNs: 978-1-9753-4316-3 (paperback)
978-1-9753-4317-0 (ebook)

10 9 8 7 6 5 4 3 2 1

LSC-C

Printed in the United States of America

I KEPT PRESSING THE

100-MILLION-YEAR

BUTTON

AND CAME OUT ON TOP

~THE UNBEATABLE REJECT SWORDSMAN~

4

CHAPTER 1

Darkness & The Sword Master Festival

It was the morning after my fight with the Black Organization. Lia and I were dragging our heavy-limbed and exhausted bodies to the 1-A classroom.

"*Hraah*... I'm so tired, Allen," Lia said, putting her hand to her mouth to stifle an adorable yawn.

"Yeah, me too," I responded.

Lia had been confined in a cell for an entire day, and I had extinguished all my strength in my life-and-death battle with Zach Bombard. We'd only gotten a few hours of sleep, and neither of us felt like ourselves.

We arrived at the 1-A classroom and opened the door.

"Hey, it's Lia!"

"Thank goodness you're okay!"

"That must have been really hard on you. I'm glad to see you're safe!"

Everyone in the class rushed toward Lia the moment they saw her.

"Sorry for worrying you all. Allen came to save me right away, so I was unhurt in the end," she said.

The door opened creakily behind us to reveal Rose, looking even more tired than usual.

"Good morning, Rose," I said.

"Morning, Rose... This has to be your worst bedhead yet," observed Lia.

"...G'mornin'," Rose responded drowsily. Hair standing up every which way, she staggered through the classroom and plopped down into her seat. All three of us were dealing with extreme exhaustion from the previous day's adversities.

We made casual conversation until the *ding-dong-ding-dong* of the bell announced the start of class.

"Good morning, boys and girls! What a beautiful day this is!"

Chairwoman Reia threw the classroom door open, energetic as ever. *Her stamina is inhuman,* I thought. Unlike us, she didn't look remotely tired.

"Hmm, do we have anything to discuss during morning home-room...? Not especially. Let's make today a great one! We're starting with Soul Attire class for first period. Meet up in the Soul Attire Room right away!" the chairwoman announced, enthusiastically clapping her hands.

■

After moving to the Soul Attire Room, we each grabbed one soul-crystal sword and initiated a dialogue with our Spirit Cores.

Man... It feels like it's been ages since I've done this. It hadn't actually been very long since I last went to the Soul World, but it felt like it had been forever with everything that had happened since then.

All right, let's do this... I gripped my soul-crystal sword tight with both hands and concentrated my consciousness into the depths of my soul. I sank deeper and deeper, and when I opened my eyes, I saw a sprawling wasteland. Rotten trees. Rotten earth. Rotten air. Everything in *his* world was rotten.

A giant boulder with cracks on its surface towered in front of me, and *he* was sitting cross-legged on top of it.

"Haah... You never learn, do you...? Have you still not wrapped your puny brain around the idea that you can't beat me no matter how many times you try, peabrain? Huh?" he said, sighing in frustration.

"I'll challenge you as many times as it takes. Who says I'll never be able to beat you?" I responded.

"Were you dropped on your head as a baby? A runt like you could never hope to win against me. Got that?"

He made no effort to hide his displeasure, and the malice in his demeanor made my hair stand on end.

"We won't know that until we try, right?" I challenged brazenly in an effort to keep from being overwhelmed, and his malicious aura vanished.

"...Whatever. I was itchin' for a little exercise today anyway, so I'll give you a shot." He stood up leisurely, and a pitch-black darkness flowed from his entire body.

"What the—?!" I shouted.

"What're you so surprised about...? This was *my* power in the first place. You've gotten a little bit stronger, which has given me some of my strength back," he revealed to me with a wicked smile.

It wasn't his use of the darkness that surprised me. *It's so much denser than mine!* I was surprised because of how absurdly different his darkness was from what I produced. Its density, volume, and force were overwhelming. It was on another level. The power I'd stolen from him last night was only a tiny piece of it.

"Crap..."

I focused my mind and tried to summon the ebon blade I had used the night before. But it didn't appear. "Huh...?" The only thing that emerged from my hand was a thin, black mist.

"Ha! You clueless brat... You just materialized my black sword in your last fight. You're all out of spirit power."

"S-spirit power? What's that?" I asked, confused by the unfamiliar term.

"Ask Black Fist!" he shouted, and leaped at me explosively.

"Dammit..." Left with no choice, I gave up on manifesting the ebon blade and drew my own sword. Unfortunately, I acted too late.

"What are you looking at, dumbass?" I heard his cold voice from behind me.

H-how is he so fast?! Enshrouded in the darkness, he was significantly faster than he had ever been.

"Plant your feet, wimp!"

"Whuh?!"

He was also much more powerful than before. *Where is this strength coming from...?* I managed to block his powerful kick with my sword, but I was sent flying anyway, hitting the ground hard and skidding until my back slammed into the giant boulder.

"Gah..." My consciousness wavered after the impact, and my weapon slipped from my hand. *Defending myself is pointless...* The defensive techniques I had acquired were ineffectual in the face of his relentless assault.

"You're done."

I heard his emotionless voice from above my head before he swung at me with a low punch.

"Crap... *I...won't...lose!*" I shouted. I thrust out both hands to meet his approaching fist, and something strange happened—a circle of darkness appeared and blocked his blow completely.

I stared, wide-eyed in disbelief. *H-hey, this means...!* Until now, I hadn't had any means of defending against his attacks. Meeting his blows with my sword or defending myself with my arms did nothing to quell his might, and I always ended up seriously injured. This time, however, I'd stopped his punch completely. It was the first time I had ever successfully defended against his attack.

So the darkness can be used for defense! Having successfully controlled the darkness for the first time, I clenched my fists with renewed determination.

"Tch, don't get cocky, you little twerp!"

He kicked me hard in the side with a leg coated in darkness.

"Gah!" I was knocked down and sent rolling on the ground. "*Blargh...* haah, haah..." Blood rushed to my head and intense pain racked my entire body.

"Ha... Ha-ha-ha!" I laughed. A strong sense of satisfaction overcame me. *This is great... I can get even stronger!* Mastering this darkness could let me reach even greater heights as a swordsman! *It'll also enable me to draw more power from* him...*and maybe even realize my Soul Attire like everyone else in my class!*

This was a fruitful trip—I'd learned how to control the darkness and had found out about the term "spirit power." Satisfied, I was returned to the real world.

■

I headed right for Chairwoman Reia once I woke up.

"Chairwoman, can I ask a question?" I said.

"Of course. You can ask me anything," she answered.

"Thank you. Um…what is 'spirit power'?" I asked.

"Hmm… Where did you hear about that?" The chairwoman responded with a question of her own, looking a little surprised.

"I heard it just now—my Spirit Core let it slip when we were about to fight in the Soul World."

"Hm, I see… How should I handle this…?" she mused, scratching her cheek with an uneasy expression. "I had been thinking about discussing spirit power once you all hit the wall, but…yeah, this'll work. Rose and a number of other students are already having trouble making progress, so I guess it would be best to explain it now."

The chairwoman nodded after coming to that conclusion.

"It's important that I be fair with this… All right! I'll explain spirit power to the whole class in second period! Sorry, Allen, but can you wait just a little bit longer?"

"Yes, ma'am, that's no problem."

Sure enough, it sounded like spirit power would be an important component for getting stronger. While I had her attention, I decided to ask another question that had been bothering me all day.

"Sorry, Chairwoman… Can I ask one more question?"

"Yeah, go ahead."

"Um, well… Lia's father—er, the king of Vesteria—is really mad, isn't he?"

No restrictions had been put in place to keep what happened yesterday under wraps. That meant King Gris had certainly already heard about the Black Organization's abduction of Lia. *He dotes on her like no father I've ever seen.* There was no doubt that he was seething with rage right now.

"Ah, about that..." The chairwoman paused, looking troubled, before she continued in a whisper. "Just between us... He hasn't said a word."

"...What?"

"There's no way he could have missed an incident that big. He has to know that Lia was kidnapped, but he hasn't uttered a single complaint. It's unsettling. What's going on with that guy?"

"That *is* weird..."

Reia's account didn't mesh with my impression of the king at all. I would have thought he'd bombard the country of Liengard with a string of angry phone calls and start an all-out war with the Black Organization the moment he heard the news of his daughter's kidnapping. *What in the world is going on?* I wondered.

"Anyway, things concerning Lia have settled down for now. I don't know what's going to happen from here on out, but there's not much point in worrying about it at the moment," Chairwoman Reia said with a shrug.

"Yeah..."

Fretting over something we wouldn't find any answers for would get us nowhere. What I needed to do was prepare myself for anything, and focus on what I could do for now. That was the best mindset to have.

"Thank you, Chairwoman. I'm gonna dive back in!"

I went back to the Soul World and challenged *him* again and again until first period ended.

■

First period seemed to go by in a flash. We took a short break, and the moment the chime for the start of second period rang, Chairwoman Reia blew her favorite whistle.

"Listen up, boys and girls! I have something to tell you about, so gather around."

Everyone in the class crowded around her, looking puzzled by her sudden summons.

"I know this is sudden, but I want each and every one of you to measure your spirit power! You may be wondering right now—*What's spirit power?* Well don't worry, I've got you covered!" she began before continuing in a booming voice. "Spirit power is essentially your mental energy. We swordfighters expend it to realize our powerful Soul Attire. Let's see... You know how you always feel mentally exhausted at the end of Soul Attire class? That's because you've spent a lot of spirit power, and have little mental energy left."

Reia continued after a short pause.

"Spirit power isn't something you're born with but is rather something you acquire through raining with your Soul Attire. There is technically no limit to the heights you can grow your spirit power to, although that is very unlikely to matter. It increases bit by bit the more you train... But it's not like people can live for hundreds of millions of years. So while there's no limit to your spirit power in theory, there may as well be because of our biological limitations as humans. That's the gist of spirit power," she finished. "Let's get to measuring! Follow me!"

We walked briskly through the expansive Soul Attire Room. After about three minutes, double doors roughly two meters tall came into view. *I had no idea these doors were here...* They blended almost completely into the wall, so I had never noticed them.

"Here we go!" The chairwoman opened the doors and entered, students trailing behind her. Inside the room, an intricate and fantastical magic circle was scrawled across the floor.

"This is the Spirit Power Room. As the name implies, it was constructed to measure the spirit power of swordsmen. They say 'a picture is worth a thousand words,' so I'll give you a quick demonstration," the chairwoman said. She cracked her neck, then strode into the middle of the magic circle. "Whoo..." She let out a large breath, and the magic circle lit up with a crimson light.

""""Whoa!"""" A number of students gasped at the mystical sight.

"Ahem... The color the magic circle lights up with is determined by the amount of spirit power you possess. In order of least to most spirit power, the colors are purple, indigo, blue, green, yellow, orange, and red. For reference, let me think… For first years at your current stage, indigo and above would be considered excellent."

The chairwoman stepped away from the magic circle after finishing her demonstration.

"Measuring is very easy. Just move to the center of the magic circle and focus your consciousness into the depths of your soul. Your spirit power will then be automatically analyzed. Okay, everyone feeling ready can go ahead and start measuring themselves!" she encouraged, clapping her hands and passing the baton to the students.

"All right, I'll go first!"

Tessa Balmond, practitioner of the Slice Iron Style, volunteered enthusiastically.

"Awesome. Step right up. Remember, what you want to do is sink your consciousness into the depths of your soul, just like you do when you converse with your Spirit Core," Chairwoman Reia explained.

"Got it!" he replied cheerfully, stepping into the magic circle. A moment after he closed his eyes, an indigo light glowed beneath his feet.

"Wow, indigo already! That's amazing, Tessa!" said the surprised chairwoman after a gasp of admiration.

"Heh-heh, thank you!" Tessa responded.

We then measured ourselves one by one. Most of us were purple, though the occasional student got indigo. Rose ended up getting blue. Remarkably, Lia got green. Taken aback by this, the chairwoman praised her profusely, saying that she "should have expected no less from the talent that will inherit Vesteria."

Rose seemed quite disappointed that her spirit power was inferior to Lia's. "I-impressive…," she mumbled, trembling slightly.

Shortly afterward, my turn finally arrived.

"You're the last one, Allen. Give it a shot," instructed the chairwoman.

"Yes, ma'am," I responded. I stepped into the center of the magic circle, let out a large breath, and concentrated my mind. "Hoo… Haa…" I plunged my consciousness deeper and deeper into my soul, until something unexpected happened.

"…?!"

The magic circle glowed with an unnaturally dark luminescence, then shattered with a high-pitched *crack*.

■

I stood dumbfounded within the shattered magic circle.

"H-huh...?"

"""" """"
......

The room was filled with shocked silence. The gazes of my classmates pierced my body, and an uncomfortable sweat broke out across my back.

Uh... This was my fault, wasn't it? Thirty people measured their spirit power before me, but this hadn't happened to any of them. Maybe I screwed up the process somehow.

As the uncomfortable silence persisted, an anxious thought crossed my mind: *How much did this magic circle cost?* Accident or not, I had just broken school equipment. Naturally, I would have to pay for it.

The academy had gone out of its way to install the magic circle in a room made specifically for its use. There was no way this thing's price tag topped out at only one or two thousand guld. *Oh yeah... Aren't the soul-crystal swords a million guld each?* There were over one hundred soul-crystal swords stored in the prep room, but there was only one magic circle. There had to be a reason for that scarcity.

It'll be at least more than one million guld... That's for sure... I felt blood drain from my face. That was a lot of money, enough to live comfortably for a year without working a day. *This is bad.* I was supposed to become a great swordsman so I could give Mom an easy life... Now I was going to get trapped in an unending cycle of debt.

N-no, calm down! There's a chance that it could be surprisingly cheap! I didn't have any proof it was that expensive yet. There was even a chance it was a consumable item with a limited number of uses! Clinging to that faint hope, I glanced at the chairwoman.

"Wh-what in the world?!" she gasped, wide-eyed with trembling fists.

...I'm done for. She looked rattled; there was no doubt about it now. The magic circle had to be significantly rarer and more expensive than the soul-crystal swords.

Are you kidding me...? Allen can't even be measured?! Did he inter-fere somehow? ...No, that's impossible. I've never heard of a Spirit Core affecting spirit power readings. That means the magic circle was broken by Allen's monstrous spirit power alone... thought Reia.

I worked up the courage to speak to the chairwoman, who was still standing there silent and pale-faced.

"Ch-Chairwoman...?"

She didn't reply to my question. The shock must have been too great. She was chewing her lip, apparently lost in thought.

His spirit power must have ballooned this large because of that cursed 100-Million-Year Button... I'll bet he was confined in the World of Time for ages. Maybe even for a thousand years, or if he had a really rough time, two thousand years... Poor thing. It must have taken him forever to break out.

The chairwoman recovered from her shock and stared at me intently. "Allen, how many years—"

"I-I'm sorry," I apologized, bowing my head forcefully. The chairwoman looked bewildered.

"Wh-what are you apologizing for?" she asked.

"I'm sorry for breaking the magic circle. I don't have the money right now, but I'll work as hard as I can to pay it off—"

"Ah, don't worry about that. These magic circles are made with low-quality soul crystals that can't be used for soul-crystal swords. They're not very pricey," she interjected.

"R-really?!"

"Yeah. Also, the accident occurred during class. It's not your responsibility, so you don't need to pay for it. You can relax."

"Th-thank goodness..."

I sighed with great relief.

"Ch-Chairwoman Reia! What does this say about Allen's spirit power?! You didn't mention black light in your explanation!" Lia hounded the chairwoman.

"I've never seen black light either, so I can't say for sure, but...one thing is certain: Allen's spirit power is greater than anyone else's in this room. Including mine."

"""Huh?!"""" my classmates exclaimed, freezing up. Chairwoman Reia's personality was problematic in many respects, but her strength in combat was undeniable. Everyone gasped at the revelation that my spirit power was greater than hers.

"Ch-Chairwoman... That has to be an exaggeration, right?" I asked timidly.

"Nope, it's the truth. You surpass me when it comes to spirit power. You should be proud. There aren't many swordfighters in the world who possess spirit power as vast as yours," she answered with a smile and a thumbs-up.

"Th-thank you so much!"

I was overjoyed. In my fifteen years of life, I had never once been praised by a teacher for my skill as a swordsman. It was certainly never going to happen at Grand Swordcraft Academy.

You have no talent, Allen. No amount of practice swings will make any difference. Go ahead and quit—I'm sick of seeing your face. Those were the kinds of things my teachers told me with cold, emotionless eyes.

Now I had just been praised as a swordsman, and while attending an Elite Five Academy, a much more prestigious school than Grand Swordcraft Academy, no less. Better still, the praise had come from Chairwoman Reia, aka the Black Fist, who was recognized the world over for her incredible talent as a swordswoman!

I had no idea being complimented would make me this happy... I thought, basking in great joy.

"Wh-whoa now... Does he really have more spirit power than Black Fist?!"

"That means he has the spirit power to match a nation's army, right?"

"You're amazing, Allen!"

My classmates praised me openly as well. Once everyone quieted down, the chairwoman clapped her hands.

"Okay, we're done measuring, so I'm now going to teach you a tried-and-true training method to strengthen your spirit power." She cleared her throat and continued. "The method is extremely simple. All you have to do is push yourself to your absolute limit! Wear down your mental energy until the moment your soul begins to cry out in pain, and your spirit power will grow significantly! You can do practice swings, run laps—it doesn't matter how you do it! Just find a grueling routine that makes you want to scream, and repeat it over and over again!"

Find a grueling routine that makes you want to scream, and repeat it over and over again. This training method was made for me. I had swung my sword single-mindedly for over a billion years when I was in the World of Time. I was already more than accustomed to the monotonous and arduous patience, endurance, and repetition this training would require. Lately, I had even come to enjoy this kind of thing.

I'd probably gained my massive spirit power from my experience in that world.

"Let's see...we still have thirty minutes until the end of second period. Let's return to the Soul Attire Room and resume class! I'm going to have you all work on strengthening your spirit power with physical training this afternoon!" Chairwoman Reia announced.

""Yes, ma'am!"" we all responded.

After learning about spirit power, an essential aspect of training our Soul Attire, we once again began our dialogues with our Spirit Cores.

■

Once second period ended, Lia, Rose, and I grabbed lunch and gathered in front of the Student Council room. We were there to participate in the "regular meeting," which was really nothing more than a casual lunch gathering.

I knocked gently on the door.

"Come in," answered Shii in a dignified voice. I opened the door, and she rushed forward the moment she saw it was us. "Allen, Rose... And Lia! I'm so glad you're all safe!" She squeezed Lia's hands with a look of true relief on her face.

"You've had it rough."

"I'm relieved you look okay, though!"

Lilim and Tirith shared kind words as well.

"Sorry for worrying you all," Lia responded, bowing her head in apology.

"You are not to blame. The fault lies at the feet of my family for allowing

such dangerous criminals to infiltrate the country. I am so sorry...,"
Shii said, bowing her head apologetically. She was a member of House
Arkstoria, one of the leading families in the government of this country.

"Y-you don't have to apologize, President! Please, raise your head!"
said Lia.

"Handling matters of national defense is one of House Arkstoria's
most important duties. We have no excuses for allowing this to tran-
spire...," the president insisted before she faced me and Rose. "Allen,
Rose, we are in your debt. If anything had happened to Lia...it would
have been a problem for more than just House Arkstoria. It likely would
have developed into a national incident."

"I was only saving my friend. Don't worry about it," I responded.

"Yeah, same for me," agreed Rose.

Shii muttered a brief thanks and began to explain the state of the
country's defenses.

"Under House Arkstoria's guidance, national security has been tight-
ened more than ever before. We also plan to increase border personnel
starting next month. It won't be so easy to slip inside our country from
now on," she claimed.

A momentary silence befell us.

"Anyway, that's enough serious talk! Let's eat lunch!" Lilim urged.

"I'm absolutely starving...," Tirith added.

The two upperclassmen tactfully lifted the gloomy mood.

"Yeah, I'm getting hungry, too," I said, taking the opportunity to
enjoy lunch with everyone.

"...Yes, you're right. Let's start our regular Student Council meeting!"
Shii responded with a small, cheerful smile, picking up on our intention.

We had our usual lunch meeting and steered clear of discussing anything serious.

■

After attending the Student Council meeting and afternoon physical
training, I went to the chairwoman's office. I knocked on the dignified
black door three times.

"Enter," Chairwoman Reia responded stiffly.

...I know that voice. I had known the chairwoman for long enough now to realize what her tone meant. *She sounds stiff, but somewhat cheerful as well. I'm sure she's slacking off...* She had probably forced her work onto Eighteen so she could read her favorite magazine, *Weekly Shonen Blade.*

I opened the door and saw Reia sitting behind her luxurious black desk, wearing a serious expression.

"...I'm not at a good stopping place right now, so please wait over there for a bit," she requested without even bothering to glance at me. She furrowed her brow as she ran her eyes through the magazine she was holding.

"Yes, ma'am," I responded shortly, and waited for her to finish. It took about three minutes.

"Phew...," she sighed, dropping *Weekly Shonen Blade* on the desk after thoroughly devouring the section she was reading. Her face was alight with excitement. This week's issue must have been exciting. "That was *so gooood*," she said to herself earnestly before downing a glass of water on her desk.

"So, do you need something, Allen? It's rare for you to visit my office alone," she asked.

"Yes, ma'am. Honestly, I would like your advice on something...," I responded.

"Oh really. You can ask me anything. I happen to have lots of free time today."

"Thank you. So basically..." I began to tell the chairwoman about the numerous issues that I had been stressing over—how I was suddenly unable to manifest the black sword that I summoned at the research facility; how *he* had told me in the Soul World that I was all out of spirit power; and how I had gained a little bit of control over the darkness. She listened to everything quietly.

"Hmm... From how I understand it, you're not sure about the order in which you should train to summon the black sword, grow your spirit power, and increase your control of the darkness, or how to go about any of it," she said, accurately summarizing what I had been struggling with.

"Yes, that's exactly right," I responded.

Between the ebon blade, the existence of spirit power, and the darkness, I had learned a lot in just a few days. The only way to materialize the black sword—to produce my Soul Attire—was to defeat *him* in the Soul World. The chairwoman had said that the best way to strengthen spirit power was straightforward physical exercise. But I had no idea what to do to gain full control over the darkness. Honestly, I didn't even know where to start.

"Of the three steps you mentioned, you should definitely start by training the darkness," the chairwoman declared confidently.

"Really?" I responded.

"Yeah, absolutely. Gaining full command of it should be your top priority. After that, you should focus on strengthening your spirit power to increase the volume of darkness you can control. And lastly, you should train to manifest the black sword, which is likely your Soul Attire. That sounds like the best order to me."

"O-okay, that makes sense!"

First, I needed to master my control of the darkness, and then train my spirit power to increase its volume. Once I had accomplished that, I needed to train to become as strong as possible so I could defeat *him* and manifest my Soul Attire. That definitely sounded logical.

"That helps a lot. Thank you very much!" I said graciously.

"*Haah*...you're welcome. The Sword Master Festival is almost here. I'll be cheering you on from the sidelines," the chairwoman assured.

"I'll do my best!" I replied energetically. "Have a nice day, Chairwoman."

"Don't push yourself too hard."

I left her office.

■

Reia watched Allen go.

"...Okay, I probably saved a little time with that," Reia muttered, feeling incredibly guilty.

"Are you sure it was all right telling him that, Mistress Reia? That training regimen is clearly going to get him nowhere," asked Eighteen, who had been slaving away at paperwork in the corner of the room.

"…"

Reia fell silent with an expression of shame on her face. Her conscience was killing her for what she just did.

"What he should clearly do first is work to acquire the black sword. The darkness is nothing more than a byproduct. Spending any time trying to strengthen it is just going down an unnecessary detour… The black sword is clearly his Soul Attire, and he will never obtain it by following your instructions. There is no way you don't know that, Mistress," Eighteen continued.

Reia sighed loudly in response to Eighteen's honest opinion.

"I didn't have a choice. I never thought Allen would wrestle power from him so quickly… *Nobody* saw this coming," she said, shaking her head hopelessly. "Allen is an undeniable prodigy. He forced that monster into submission with his mental fortitude… Honestly, I don't know which of them is the monster anymore."

Reia smiled wryly.

"Anyway, we can't let Allen stand out any more than he already has. There'll be big trouble if the Black Organization's top brass takes an interest in him. Especially the Thirteen Oracle Knights—I don't know what would happen if one came looking for him," she finished with a shrug.

"I see… Am I correct to deduce that you are prioritizing keeping Master Allen hidden?"

"Yeah, that's right."

"I understand. But if that is the case, then what about his participation in the Sword Master Festival?"

"There's no way he'll achieve any growth from such a nonsensical training regimen. I'm sure he'll get crushed miserably once he faces a student from another Elite Five Academy. Actually, we'd better pray that's what happens. The Sword Master Festival gets a hell of a lot of attention…," Reia said, seeming to lose herself in thought for a moment. "Anyway, that's enough talk! Stop running your mouth and get back to work!" She clapped her hands, and ordered Eighteen to get back to work.

"Y-yes, ma'am!"

What Reia didn't realize, however, was that she'd made a major miscalculation. By being overly cautious of Allen's talent, she'd overlooked his idiosyncrasies. From that day on, he devoted himself completely to gaining control over the darkness. He worked at it when walking, when he was in class, when he was doing practice swings, when he was eating, when he was in the bath—he spent his every waking moment intently grappling with the darkness. This was all possible thanks to the endurance he'd gained from overcoming one billion years of hardship in the world of time.

And finally—the day of the Sword Master Festival arrived.

■

I devoted myself to the brilliant training regimen Chairwoman Reia recommended to me and spent each and every day working hard to increase my control over the darkness. Practicing with a clear goal in mind, instead of aimlessly swinging my sword like I usually did, made it feel fresh and fun.

I spent my days in class. I spent my after-school hours training with the Practice-Swing Club. At night I worked with Lia and Rose to polish our swordcraft. I remained conscious of the darkness throughout that entire daily routine.

And now, it was finally the first day of the Sword Master Festival.

"I'm heading out, Lia." It was seven in the morning. After finishing my morning routine, I called out to Lia by the door.

"Be careful out there. I'll be cheering for you in the stands, so make sure you find me, okay?" she responded.

"Sure thing."

The participants in the Sword Master Festival were required to arrive at the venue slightly earlier than everyone else. That's why I was leaving the dorm before her.

"Good luck, Allen."

"Thanks."

Lia waved as I left, and I headed right for the Student Council room. The plan was to walk to the venue with the whole team after holding a quick strategy meeting. I gently knocked on the door when I arrived, and after receiving permission to enter, I walked into the room.

"Good morning President, Lilim, and Tirith," I said.

"Good morning, Allen," the president responded.

"Good morning, Allen! Isn't the weather just perfect today for the Sword Master Festival?"

"...Mornin'."

Shii smiled kindly, Lilim was her usual bundle of energy, and Tirith was drowsy as she always was in the morning. They each greeted me in their own distinct way.

"Let's get started on our strategy meeting now that Allen's here," the president said.

"Yeah, let's do it! I say we *attack, attack, attack!*"

"Can we keep this short...? *Yawn...*"

I involuntarily chuckled at how typical those responses were of Lilim and Tirith.

"Oh yeah, before that... I haven't shown this to you yet, Allen. This is our roster," the president said, handing me a printed sheet of paper.

"Thank you," I responded.

The names of the five Thousand Blade Academy team members were listed on the sheet in fighting order.

> First: Allen Rodol
> Second: Lilim Chorine
> Third: Tirith Magdarote
> Vice-Captain: Shii Arkstoria
> Captain: Sebas Chandler

"Who's Sebas Chandler?" I asked. That was the one name I was unfamiliar with.

"Sebas Chandler is the vice president of our club," Shii answered with a sigh.

"Huh? Did you find him?" I asked. If I recalled correctly, the vice president had gone to the Holy Ronelian Empire, a travel-restricted country, in search of a blood diamond. That he had apparently headed there as a result of losing a penalty game made the story even more ridiculous.

"Nope, he's still missing."

"That means…"

"Yep, we'll have to forfeit the captain's match." Shii frowned and continued speaking. "Unfortunately, there's nothing we can do about it. The head of the disciplinary committee refused to substitute due to lack of interest… That left Sebas as the only person left with the skill to serve as our captain or vice-captain. I thought betting on the off chance he returned would be better than leaving the slot blank, so I put his name down."

"Th-that makes sense…"

Duels between sword wielders were serious business. Putting someone on the roster who lacked the necessary skill could result in terrible tragedy. The captain and vice-captain of each team were the strongest duelists in their school, so the pool of candidates to fill the two positions was naturally limited.

Wait, this means that the president, as talented as she is, believes the head of the disciplinary committee and Sebas Chandler are powerful enough to deserve being the captain… I'd like to challenge them if I ever got the chance.

"That means our strategy is going to be *attack, attack, attack!* It's the only choice we have!" the president declared, pounding her desk and bringing me out of my thoughts.

"That's what I want to hear, Shii! We're on the same page!" Lilim agreed emphatically with Shii's aggressive proposal.

The president gave a satisfied nod and began to explain our straightforward strategy. "Our gameplan is extremely simple. As you can see, I stepped down from the captain position. I did that to ensure we take the vice-captain duel! That means you three need to win two of the first three bouts! We're going to secure an early victory before the captain's match can even start!"

"I-I'll do my best!" I responded.

"Don't worry about me! There's no way I'll lose!" Lilim proclaimed.

"I'll try some, I guess…" Tirith said unenthusiastically.

"Sounds like we're set! Let's head for the Sword Master Festival venue!" The president strode cheerfully out of the room, and we followed behind her.

■

The Sword Master Festival was the most popular swordcraft competition in the country, and every high school swordcraft academy participated. The tournament started with a group stage, with the academies being split into batches labeled A through H. The top two schools from each group advanced to the knockout stage.

To accommodate the scale of the tournament, the Sword Master Festival took place over three days. The group stage was on the first day, the knockout stage was on the second, and the third and final day was reserved for the championship bout.

"Okay, we're here. This is Aurest National Arena, the venue for Group A," Shii announced, pointing at a giant, circular arena in front of us.

"Wow, this is another really impressive building…," I said to myself. It was a little smaller than the Grand Coliseum in Vesteria. The modern steel frame and concrete construction of this building set it apart from the dignified, weather-worn stone of the coliseum.

"Let's go ahead through reception. We need to get comfortable with the arena," the president said before taking off for the reception tent. After registering, we headed through the gate and into the Aurest National Arena. One long stone passageway later, we were greeted by the sight of a large crowd of swordfighters.

Whoa… There were sword wielders to the left of me, to the right of me, everywhere I looked. Their presence created a sense of pressure that threatened to overwhelm me. I felt so dizzy, in fact, that I started to wonder if I had a pathological fear of crowds. My hometown of Goza Village had more livestock than people, so I didn't do well with large groups of people. However, I had no choice but to push myself to get used to it.

"Hoo… Haa…" I calmed my nerves by doing some deep breathing.

A short while later, the executive committee for the Sword Master Festival started the opening ceremony. An older man stepped up onto the stage, greeted the crowd, and explained the rules in simple terms.

Each academy was represented by a lineup of five students: the first, the second, the third, the vice-captain, and the captain. The first team to three wins was the victor. In the interest of fostering the talents of the younger students, each school was required to fill the first spot on their lineup with a first-year student. Swords were the only equipment allowed; participants were prohibited from bringing any other items, like defensive gear, with them into combat. There was nothing unusual about the rules.

"I will now reveal the bracket for today's group stage," the man said, and a bracket appeared on a giant screen behind him.

Let's see, where are we...? I examined the bracket closely and found our school on the left end. It looked like we were up first. *Our first opponent is Werewolf Academy.* I had never heard of them.

Lilim grimaced openly. "Geez, we're starting with Werewolf Academy. This sucks..."

"Have you heard of them, Lilim?"

"Yeah, they're sorta well-known. They've made it out of the group stage two years in a row, so they're definitely one to watch out for. I don't care about that, though... What gets me is how rowdy they are. I can't stand them," she answered.

"H-huh..."

Suddenly, a clear female voice reverberated throughout the arena. "We have a packed schedule today, so let's go ahead and start the first matchup of the group stage! Thousand Blade Academy and Werewolf Academy, please prepare yourselves! Everyone else, please exit the stage!"

The first match was about to begin.

"Good luck, Allen!" said Shii.

"Go get 'em! I know you can do it!" Lilim exclaimed.

"I'll be cheering you on from the sidelines...," Tirith added.

They all patted me on the back encouragingly.

"Okay! I'll give it my best shot!" I responded, pumping myself up for the duel against Werewolf Academy's first year.

■

Following the announcer's instructions, all students not belonging to the Thousand Blade and Werewolf teams filed off the stage and headed for the locker room. I glanced at the audience as the great number of students made their way.

Th-there are so many people here... The venue was sold out. I didn't see one empty seat. The Sword Master Festival truly was popular; I was amazed that even the group stage drew this much attention.

I wonder where Lia is? Picking her out in a crowd of tens of thousands of people without knowing where she was sitting was not realistic. I strained my eyes to look for her anyway and was interrupted when the announcer began to speak.

"Attention everyone! The match between Werewolf Academy and Thousand Blade Academy's first years is about to begin!" The crowd exploded with excitement, cheering loudly enough to shake the ground. "That's what I want to hear! Now that we're in the mood, it's time to introduce the participants!"

The announcer cleared her throat and began to introduce us enthusiastically.

"From one side we have the first for Werewolf Academy—Garo Yundra! According to my notes, he is a naturally gifted prodigy who manifested his Soul Attire at just ten years old! He also possesses full mastery over the Flower Garden School of Swordcraft, a famous Western style! He was accepted into an Elite Five Academy, but his application fell through after a violent incident. That means he's got the skills of an Elite Five Academy student!"

Garo Yundra walked calmly onto the stage after being introduced. He had flashy blond hair gelled perfectly into place. His handsome face was brimming with confidence. He was slightly taller than me at a little above 175 centimeters, and his Werewolf Academy uniform was made of black fabric embroidered with red crosses.

"YEEEEEAAAAHH! TEAR HIM TO SHREDS, GARO!"

"SLAUGHTER THOSE THOUSAND BLADE PUSSIES!"

"SHOW 'EM THAT THE ELITE FIVE ARE DINOSAURS!"

I heard foul-mouthed cheers from the Werewolf Academy students erupt from the crowd. They were all wearing the same uniform as Garo. *Do they have to be that vulgar, though?* It looked like Lilim was right about the academy's unsavory nature.

"Next, we have the first for Thousand Blade Academy—Allen Rodol! According to my notes, he… Huh? U-ummm… he doesn't belong to any school of swordcraft, and instead spends his days performing practice swings in total silence. As for his Soul Attire—what the…? He hasn't even manifested it yet…," the announcer trailed off.

Talk about a miserable introduction. *Everything she said was true, but surely she could've played me up a little…,* I thought.

"Pfft… Gya-ha-ha-ha-ha! He's a self-taught swordsman… that's the funniest shit I've ever heard!"

"I had they were going down the toilet, but I didn't think it would be *this* pathetic."

"Thousand Blade Academy has gone to shit! They'll get kicked out of the Elite Five Academies in no time!"

I received relentless ridicule from Werewolf Academy's spectator seating. *It's been a while since I've experienced this…* I had been making more friends lately, so I didn't have to deal with this kind of abuse as often anymore.

"I'M HERE FOR YOU, ALLEN! DON'T LET THOSE THUGS BEAT YOU!"

Just when I was starting to feel discouraged, I heard a reassuring cheer from directly behind me. *That's Lia's voice!* I spun around and saw her cheering loudly and waving at me. She was in the best seats in the venue in the very front row. Rose, Tessa, and the rest of Class 1-A were behind her, as well as many upperclassmen in Thousand Blade uniforms.

I waved back at Lia, and then realized that something felt off. *That's weird…* My classmates and the upperclassmen were being strangely silent in response to the ridicule Thousand Blade was being subjected to. Not only that—they were grinning. *What in the world are they think-ing?* I wondered in confusion.

"Hey, what're ya waitin' for? You're free to forfeit if you're too chicken," Garo said with a provoking smirk.

"No, I'm good," I responded.

I had been subjected to a miserable amount of verbal abuse during my three years at Grand Swordcraft Academy. This was nothing in comparison. *Plus, I'm not alone anymore!* Lia's voice easily outweighed the thousands of people booing me.

"Heh-heh-heh, if you say so... But hey, don't worry. I have enough honor to know I shouldn't go all out against some self-taught loser with no Soul Attire. Ha-ha-ha!" Garo howled with laughter after taunting me yet again.

As a swordsman, I couldn't let a comment like that slide. "Duels are serious. You have to give them your all."

He was right that I hadn't been accepted into any school of sword-craft and that I hadn't yet produced my Soul Attire. But I was still a swordsman. I couldn't overlook the humiliating suggestion that he would go easy on me.

"Whoa, there! Let me get this straight! You're saying a true prodigy like *me* should give my all against an untalented wimp like you? Don't get carried away, bud... I'll beat the shit out of you." Garo glared at me, now in an openly bad mood.

"H-huh..." He was clearly too stubborn for me to change his mind with words. There was only one thing I could do. *I need to turn up the heat until he's forced to get serious!* His crass insult quietly riled the com-petitive fire in my heart.

The announcer cleared her throat. "Ahem, are you both ready? The first duel between Thousand Blade Academy and Werewolf Academy starts—now!"

The moment she gave the signal, I kicked off the ground to charge toward Garo.

"...Huh?"

"...Wha?"

Suddenly, I was right in Garo's face. *What the...?!* I was only planning on approaching to see how he would react, but instead I'd charged into range to perform a finishing blow. By total accident, no less.

I had been focusing solely on increasing my control of the darkness late and hadn't performed any physical training to see how that had affected my body. It seemed that my physical abilities improved dramatically as the darkness adapted to me.

What should I do here? Slashing at an opponent who hadn't even drawn their blade would look poorly on me as a duelist. *But this is an all-out clash.* Holding back now would be an insult to Garo. *I can't attack an unarmed opponent, but I can't go easy on him, either...*

Caught between conflicting principles, I performed a front kick as a compromise. "Ha!" I struck him square on the stomach with my foot, only intending to immobilize him momentarily.

"GAAAH!" He bounced across the stone stage like a skipping stone and fell completely motionless.

"""...Huh?"""

The entirety of the Aurest National Arena fell silent at the shocking development.

"Wh-what the heck...? A-ah, sorry about that! Allen Rodol is the victor!" The announcer declared, plainly bewildered.

"""YEEEEEAAAAAAHHHHH!"""

My Thousand Blade upperclassmen cheered, making the silence feel like a distant memory.

"Did you see that, Werewolf Academy?! You've got no chance against our Emperor of Evil!"

"I can't believe he didn't even use a sword... He returned their insult with an even greater insult. You're one sick bastard, Allen!"

"Mwa-ha-ha, let's carry this momentum into the second and third matches!"

The unfortunately-worded comments of some of my excited upperclassmen sent some unsavory rumors spreading through the crowd.

"He knocked out Garo with one blow?! I thought Thousand Blade had fallen on hard times, but they've got a heck of a talent in this guy..."

"Garo's reputation is gonna be in tatters after losing to someone who didn't even touch his sword… I feel bad for him. He may never recover as a swordsman…"

"Allen Rodol, huh… He looks innocent enough, but he has the cruelty of a demon."

My unfair notoriety was beginning to spread beyond Thousand Blade to the general public.

"*Haah*, I hope no trouble comes of this…" Sighing loudly, I stepped off the stage.

Regardless, I'd achieved an impressive victory against Garo Yundra in the first duel.

◼

I joined up with my teammates by the wing of the stage.

"Impressive as always, Allen!" said the president.

"That kick was insane! That blew my mind!" exclaimed Lilim.

"You were pretty good…," added Tirith.

They were all overjoyed at my victory.

"Ah-ha-ha, thank you," I responded with a smile, then turned toward the spectator seating and accidentally locked eyes with Lia. Feeling a little awkward, I gave her a short wave. Her face lit up into a wide smile, and she waved back with both hands.

The announcer's voice sounded throughout the arena once more.

"Who could've seen that coming?! Allen Rodol may be this tournament's dark horse! Moving on, it's time to start the second duel!"

Lilim was our second, so she was up.

"Good luck, Lilim!" I said.

"You know what to do, right, Lilim? We have to take advantage of the momentum Allen created for us!" the president instructed.

"I'm gonna be really upset if you lose…," Tirith warned.

"Ha-ha-ha, I've got this!" Lilim exclaimed, and practically skipped up onto the stage.

◼

Lilim fought with a burning intensity and won her match without difficulty. The duel between both teams' thirds was next. Tirith was given a bit of a hard fight, but she managed to prevail in the end. That made three wins in the first three duels, which gave us a flawless victory over Werewolf Academy, who had gained a reputation as a powerhouse in recent years.

"Group A's first match in this year's Sword Master Festival is in the books! The winner is one of the Elite Five Academies, Thousand Blade Academy!" the announcer proclaimed.

"They didn't look half bad! Those were all good duels!"

"Is this the return of the unbeatable Thousand Blade?!"

The crowd exploded with deafening applause and shouts of congratulations.

"It's time to move on to the second match, Twilight Academy versus Fog Island Academy! Thousand Blade and Werewolf students, please return to the participant locker room!"

We followed the announcer's instructions and headed for the locker room. One long hallway later, I opened the door to the locker room to find all of the students inside glaring at me.

"..."

Some glanced at me out of the corner of their eyes, others gave me appraising glances, and the rest stared at me openly without even trying to hide it.

I-is it just my imagination, or...? I thought uncomfortably.

"Hmm-hmm, they've all taken great interest in you, Allen," remarked Shii.

"That was a stunning Sword Master Festival debut, after all! Man, I'm jealous!" added Lilim.

"Do they have to stare *that* much, though? It's really annoying...," complained Tirith.

My teammates laughed off the stares.

"You don't have to pay them any mind. Just relax and prepare yourself for the next match," the president advised.

"Thank you, I'll do that," I responded.

We passed the time with chatting away like we always did and waited for our second match.

■

We racked up win after win with the unstoppable momentum of a tidal wave as the group stage continued, closing out almost every match in the first three duels. Lilim and Tirith lost occasionally, but the president always clutched a win in her vice-captain duels, and we eventually advanced to the Group A finals.

"We've reached the last match of the day! The Group A finals between Thousand Blade Academy and Astral Academy are about to begin!" the announcer began in her loudest voice yet. "The top two academies from each group advance to the Sword Master Festival's knockout stage, so both of these teams have already advanced. However, this match will determine if they emerge from the group in first or second place, dramatically impacting the difficulty of their path moving forward!"

After a short pause, she continued.

"The academy that finishes with the number one seed gets to face a number two seed from another group! The academy that finishes with the number two seed has to face a number one seed from another group! That means that Thousand Blade Academy and Astral Academy will both want to secure this first-place finish!"

I was unaware of how teams were divided up in the knockout stage until that explanation. *So that's why the group stage finals are important... We can't lose here.* There was a very high chance that Ice King Academy and the other Elite Five Academies would be number one seeds. We were going to run into an Elite Five Academy eventually if we continued to win, but the later that happened, the better.

The first three matches of the knockout stage take place in just one day... Provided we continued to win, we would have to fight in three rounds tomorrow: the round of sixteen, the quarterfinals, and the semifinals. Each match was going to be brutally difficult and take a great physical toll on us. *Given the tournament format of the knockout stage and the lack of downtime between rounds, it would be best to fight the Elite Five Academies as late as possible to avoid unnecessary wear and tear.*

The announcer brought me out of my thoughts by moving on to the participant introductions.

"First up, we have the first from Thousand Blade Academy—Allen Rodol! He is undefeated so far, and even more stunningly, he hasn't even taken a single blow! This kid is undoubtedly the dark horse of the tournament!"

She jumped into the next introduction without a moment's delay.

"Next we have the first for Astral Academy—Sven Rodrick! He belongs to the rare Gentle Sword Style that originated in the south, and like Allen, he boasts an incredible undefeated record thus far!"

Sven Rodrick had long black hair that extended down both sides of his head, and a calm visage that made him look three years older than he really was. He was the same height as me at about 170 centimeters. His Astral Academy uniform looked regal and was white with yellow trim.

He walked onto the stage, then gave me a firm look as he held out his right hand. "I'm Sven Rodrick. It's nice to meet you."

"Hello, Sven. It's nice to meet you, too," I responded, exchanging a firm handshake with him before the match.

He has an honest look in his eyes. He's polite, too. It felt like this was going to be a pleasant bout.

"You've had a really rough time at school...," Sven said out of the blue, still gripping my right hand.

"...Huh?" I responded in confusion.

"Ah, sorry. I have an ability that I suppose would be best described as a byproduct of my Soul Attire. I can vicariously experience someone's life by gripping their hand."

"R-really?!"

"Yeah. For example, I can see how awful a place Grand Swordcraft Academy is... You did well to emerge from that horrible environment uncorrup...ted... Wha?!" Suddenly, his face went pale, and he shook off my right hand. "*Ahhh... Ahhh...*" He started to hyperventilate, and large drops of sweat beaded his face.

Did he...just get a secondhand experience of my memories from the World of Time? If so, I had done a terrible thing to him. I didn't know how many hundreds of millions of years he'd gone through, but judging by his reaction, whatever he saw had scarred him.

...I feel so bad. I should've pulled back my hand the moment he told me about his ability.

"Are you okay, Sven?" I took a step toward him.

"*E-eeeek!* D-don't come near me, y-you monster!" All the color drained from his face before he leaped off the stage in a mad panic and fled to the locker room.

"H-huh…" Now alone on the stage, I looked around, trying to figure out what to do.

"Wh-what in the world just happened?! One moment they're shaking hands, and the next Sven is fleeing for his life! U-umm… We will need a decision from the Sword Master Festival Executive Committee, so please wait a moment!" the announcer said and left her seat momentarily.

"…"

The eyes of the tens of thousands of people in the crowd pierced me like daggers.

"That was strange… There's clearly more to this Allen Rodol than meets the eye."

"I think you're right. Sven was terrified. Allen must have threatened him somehow."

"Hold on, what if Sven was acting?"

"Why would he have done that?"

"It's simple. Allen gave him a deal. He told Sven he would pay him a huge amount of money if he threw the match."

"Oh, that makes sense!"

I couldn't really make out what the people in the audience were saying, but I got the sense that my reputation had taken a hit. *Why does this stuff always happen to me…?* And here I was thinking I would have a pleasant match for a change. I sighed miserably.

"Thank you for your patience! Whoa… The judges have decided that Allen Rodol wins the first match by default!" the announcer declared, sharing the decision of the Sword Master Festival Executive Committee.

An uproar arose from the crowd. They seemed displeased by the result.

"A-anyway! That was unexpected, but let's regroup and move on to the second duel!" the announcer said with enough enthusiasm to overcome the crowd's displeasure, and advanced the group stage to the next duel.

∎

The match with Astral Academy was cutthroat. Lilim lost a very close fight in the hard-fought second duel, and we headed into the third duel back at square one with a 1-1 tie. Fortunately, Tirith achieved a narrow victory over a formidable opponent. The president then took care of business with an easy victory in the vice-captain duel.

With the finals complete, the announcer picked up the microphone. "The winner of the hard-fought Group A is Thousand Blade Academy! Please give them a round of applause!"

We capped off our splendid performance in Group A with a first-place finish, securing a number one seed in the knockout stage.

∎

I spent some time basking in the joy of our victory in the group stage with the president and everyone else from Thousand Blade, then returned to the dorm with Lia.

"Phew, I'm a little tired...," I said, taking my shoes off at the door and stretching.

"Hmm-hmm, I'll bet. You did really great today!" Lia beamed.

"Thanks. I couldn't have done it without your support, Lia."

I sank deep into the sofa and heaved a sigh of relief. *What a busy day...* I managed to get through my matches today because I hadn't encountered my greatest weakness, ranged attack–type Soul Attire. Still, every one of my duels had been against a swordsman talented enough to represent their respective academy. I was exhausted.

I'm just gonna rest like this for just a little bit..., I thought, deciding to briefly shut my eyes on the sofa.

"Hey... All... Hey, Allen, wake up."

"...Ngh, ah. L-Lia?"

Lia was shaking my shoulders when I came to.

"Come on, Allen, you'll catch a cold if you sleep out here," she chastised.

"Oh, shoot. I'm sorry," I responded. It seemed like I had accidentally fallen asleep on the sofa. "Hrmm…" I got up and stretched to drive away my heavy drowsiness.

"I got the bath ready. Do you want to get in now, or do you want to eat first?" Lia asked. It sounded like she had gone through a lot of trouble for me while I was napping.

"Thanks. I'll get in the bath first since it's ready now."

"Okay… Make sure you don't fall asleep in there, okay?"

"Ah-ha-ha, got it."

I then enjoyed a nice bath, ate homemade ramzac that Lia had made, and got in bed at nine.

"*Hraah*… Good night, Lia…"

"Good night, Allen."

Feeling her presence beside me as always, I slowly drifted off to sleep.

■

The next day, I met up with my teammates and walked with them to the National Crusade Coliseum. Liengard had designated the building as an important cultural property, and it was only open to the public for select events such as the Sword Master Festival. The stones it had been constructed with were thick with history, and the amphitheater's presence was so majestic that it almost made me forget about Vesteria's Grand Coliseum.

"That concludes our comments for the opening ceremony. Thank you for listening."

The Sword Master Festival Executive Committee finished their long greeting, and the sold-out crowd clapped sparsely. The same woman who had served as the announcer yesterday then took over the proceedings.

"Are you all ready for the knockout stage of the Sword Master Festival? The grand battle to determine the best of the swordcraft academies is about to begin!" she proclaimed.

Thunderous applause consisting of clapping, whistling, and shouts of encouragement broke out in response. *Huh?!* This was the first time I had ever felt *pressure* from sound. It was like my skin was tingling; it was a bizarre sensation.

"Let's get right to the lottery to determine the first matchup!"

The announcer, who was holding a microphone and standing in the front row of spectator seating, produced two large boxes with the numbers "1" and "2" written on them, respectively.

"The lottery is very simple! Box One contains balls representing the academies that finished as a number one seed in their group, and Box Two contains the same for number two seeds! I'll take one ball out of each box, and those two academies will face each other!" After finishing her explanation, the announcer rolled up her right sleeve and reached into Box One. "And now, the first competitor in the hotly anticipated first match is... Wow, that didn't take long! It's one of the Elite Five Academies, Thousand Blade Academy!"

The announcer lifted a ball into the air with "Thousand Blade Academy" written on it.

"...We're going first," I said.

"We're already up. Let's give it our all!" encouraged the president.

"All right, let's kick some ass!" exclaimed Lilim.

"Come on, really? I would've rather gone somewhere in the middle, like third...," complained Tirith.

The announcer reached into Box Two without missing a beat.

"On to Box Two—it's Snowfall Academy! However, their team was so exhausted by the group stages that Snowfall Academy withdrew from the knockout stage this morning. That means Thousand Blade Academy wins by default! It's their lucky day!"

"Th-they withdrew...?" I said aloud in confusion, and the president explained the situation to me.

"They must have expended all their energy just getting out of the group stage. One or two academies drop out at the knockout stage every year for that reason."

"Ah, that makes sense."

Their matches yesterday must have been so demanding that they would have needed more than a day to recover.

"Okay, let's regroup and start the lottery for the second match!" the announcer said, reaching into Box One once again. "By the way, Snowfall Academy is currently the only institution that has withdrawn from the knockout stage. No one else will advance by default. Okay, up next is...another Elite Five Academy! It's Ice King Academy!"

Ice King Academy was very famous. Shido and Cain attended it, and Ferris Dorhein was the chairwoman.

"Facing them is an up-and-coming school that has made it to the Sword Master Festival's knockout stage just three years after its founding, Mirage Academy!"

Mirage Academy... I had never heard of them, either.

"It's time to start the first duel! Ice King Academy and Mirage Academy students, please prepare yourselves! Everyone else, make your way to your assigned spectator seats!"

We followed the announcer's orders and walked to our places. The sixteen academies in the knockout stage had been assigned to the front row of the audience.

"First, I'm going to introduce the fighters. The first for Ice King Academy is Shido Jukurius! This rare genius with the blade has been able to manifest his Soul Attire for as long as he can remember! He emerged from the group stages undefeated by using his overwhelming strength to keep his opponents at bay. This guy's been a real force to be reckoned with so far! There have been issues with his behavior, though... He received a monthlong suspension from school not too long ago for violent conduct at this year's Elite Five Holy Festival!"

Shido strolled leisurely onto the stage after his introduction.

Man, the Elite Five Holy Festival... That had only been four months ago, but it felt like a distant memory.

"Next up, we have the first for Mirage Academy—Zari Doral! I have received no information about him! What I do know is that in Group D yesterday, he was undefeated just like Shido! He is clearly a skilled swordsman worthy of this stage!"

Zari walked onto the stage in a navy-blue robe that was likely the Mirage Academy uniform. I could feel the tension from my seat when he and Shido locked eyes.

"Are you both ready? The first duel begins—now!" the announcer declared.

"Drag Below—Acid Swamp!"

Zari vigilantly summoned his Soul Attire at once and assumed the middle stance. Shido's attitude could not have been any more different. *A-ha-ha... He never changes...* He just stood there lazily without assuming any stance, holding his sword limp in his right hand.

"Prepare yourself, Shido Jukurius!"

"Huh? I don't know who the hell you are, but go ahead and try me. I'm gonna end you in one blow."

"Ha! Let's see how long that arrogance lasts! HAAAAAAA!"

Zari's roar echoed throughout the entire venue, and the duel between the firsts of Ice King and Mirage began. It wound up being horribly one-sided.

"Good lord, is that all you've got? I didn't even work up a sweat... Pathetic."

"Grr... You're not human..."

Shido had trounced Zari without even manifesting his Soul Attire.

"H-he's so strong...," I muttered. Shido had grown significantly more powerful since the last time we'd fought. His physical abilities—arm strength, leg strength, reaction speed, and everything else that served as the basis for swordcraft—were improving at an abnormal rate.

The crowd and even the announcer were taken aback by that brutal curb-stomp of a match.

"Huh?! O-oh, sorry about that. The victor is Shido Jukurius! That was a stunning performance, wasn't it...? Shido's incredible might can only be described as superhuman! Zari is an impressive swordsman as well, but it appears he falls just short of Shido's level," the announcer commented briefly on the duel. "All right, let's move on to the second bout!"

She introduced the next two students from each academy, and the second duel began.

■

In a shocking twist, Ice King Academy ended up losing to Mirage Academy.

"Wh-wh-what just happened?! Can you all believe it?! Ice King

Academy, an Elite Five Academy and one of the favorites to win the whole tournament, was just eliminated in the round of sixteen!" the announcer declared.

A loud buzz filled the entire venue. The upset had taken everyone by surprise.

I can't believe Ice King lost... Shido had dominated in his first duel, but Mirage Academy achieved impressive victories in the second, third, and vice-captain matches.

"Ha-ha, is Shido the only competent swordsman they have?! Ice King Academy is a joke! Have their second and third years ever even held a blade? Yo, Shido—leave that small-time academy behind and transfer to Mirage!" mocked Rahm Riot, who had just won the vice-captain duel for Mirage Academy.

Th-this is bad... There was one thing I learned about Shido during our joint summer training camp with Ice King Academy: *Despite how he looks, he is very protective of his friends.* Though outwardly rude, he was nice at his core, and there was no way he was going to sit idly as his teammates were insulted.

My bad feeling was right on the money.

"Hey, you... Wanna repeat that?" said Shido, clearly offended, as he approached Rahm.

"S-stop! Don't let him get to you, Shido!" The Ice King upperclassmen tried desperately to calm Shido down. All hope of that fell apart when Rahm added fuel to the fire by provoking him further.

"Ha-ha, I'll say it as many times as you want! Ice King is a talentless dump of an academy!"

"Ahh, so you want to die, do you...? I'll grant your wish. Consume—Ice Wolf Vanargand!"

An intense cold enveloped the venue.

"Ha, how funny! A first-year brat thinks he can take a third year like me? I'm gonna show your sorry ass just what that two-year difference means! Pierce—Snake Venom!"

A surprise off-stage fight had just begun.

■

Between Shido's ability to manipulate cold air and Rahm's ability to manipulate poison, the clash between the pair of students quickly ramped up in intensity.

"Freezing Spear!" Shido rained ice spears down upon Rahm.

"Ha, predictable! Snake Coil!" Rahm easily blocked the ice spears with a purple shield made out of poison. "Let's see if you can handle this: Snake Wave!" He vigorously swung his sword, and over a hundred snakes made of poison charged at Shido.

"The hell do you think that's gonna do? Heavenly Ice Pillar!"

A frozen pillar that seemed to reach the heavens emerged from the stage to wipe out the approaching snakes.

A-amazing..., I thought. It was an evenly matched, seesaw affair. A couple minutes later, however, a clear shift was visible in both fighters.

"Somethin' the matter? Is this all the vice-captain of Mirage Academy has?!" mocked Shido.

"You goddamn brat...," responded Rahm in frustration.

Now that Shido had finished warming up, his moves were rapidly becoming more refined. Conversely, Rahm was visibly slowing. I looked closely and saw that his limbs had turned a light shade of purple, which was a sign of hypothermia.

That's happening much faster to Rahm than it did to me when I fought him... It had only been a few minutes since the two of them started fighting. Vanargand's glacial air had grown significantly stronger. *I can't believe it's that cold, though.*

Rahm was a far cry from an unskilled swordsman. His swordcraft was sharp, he was pretty athletic, and his Soul Attire was powerful and practical. *His trash talk earlier exposed some clear character flaws, but...* From a talent perspective, he was more than worthy of the Sword Master Festival's knockout stage.

Shido just happened to be an elite swordsman who greatly surpassed him. He was naturally gifted with overwhelming physical might, and his unrivaled Soul Attire—Ice Wolf Vanargand—complemented that perfectly. *He really is one of a kind...*

The duel continued to shift in Shido's favor until one of his ice spears finally pierced Rahm through the right leg.

"Ngh—gah…!" He fell to the ground clutching his leg.

There goes his mobility. That's the match… A wicked smile formed on Shido's face. Anyone could see this was over.

But Rahm wasn't ready to throw in the towel.

"This'll teach you to let your guard down, you punk! Snake Bite!" he yelled, suddenly jumping up and sending a giant snake made of a colossal amount of poison at Shido.

"Close off eternity—Frozen Waterfall!"

Unfortunately for Rahm, Shido was ready, and he summoned untold layers of thin ice to block the snake's path.

"I-impossible!" Rahm had unleashed the snake from extremely close range and with perfect timing, but it crumbled against the frigid wall.

"Good lord… Was that supposed to be a surprise attack? Pathetic."

Shido snapped his fingers, and the Frozen Waterfall broke into countless shards of ice that bore down on Rahm.

"Gah, agh…"

The avalanche of ice chunks sent him bounding across the stage painfully.

Shido's never been one to show an ounce of mercy… Rahm had severe frostbite, his right leg had been pierced, and he was bruised all over his body. His heavy injuries had clearly booked him a ticket to the hospital.

"Wh-wh-what the heck just happened?! I don't think anyone saw that fight coming! Shido Jukurius is the victor in the surprise duel between Ice King's first and Mirage's vice-captain!" the announcer proclaimed.

"This Shido kid is really good!"

"Never thought I'd see a first year beat a vice-captain…"

"It looks like we can expect great things from Ice King at next year's Sword Master Festival!"

The spectators couldn't contain their excitement at the entertaining, unscheduled fight.

The battle was over; at least, that's what everyone thought. I, however, felt a strong sense of unease. *There's more where that came from…* Once Shido's temper flared like this, simply defeating his opponent wasn't enough.

My hunch proved correct. Shido approached the motionless Rahm and readied Vanargand. *Is he performing Vanar Thrust?!* The technique was a deadly, explosively fast thrust that spewed cold air. Rahm would literally be cut to pieces if he took a blow from it in his immobilized state.

"Wait, Shido?! Stop right there! You're breaking the rules of the tournament!" the announcer hastily warned, but it was too late.

"Vanar Thrust!"

Violently cold air swept around Shido as he began the tremendously powerful thrust.

"SHIDO, NO!" I screamed.

""""Gravity Square!""""

Just then, four transparent green boards as tall as a person manifested and pinned Shido down from all sides.

"What the hell?!" Immobilized by the force of the boards, Shido gritted his teeth, veins building in his forehead.

Wh-who did that?! I looked toward the voices and saw four senior holy knights. They were walking onto the stage holding green longswords, which must have been their Soul Attire. *Senior holy knights… Thank goodness.* They had probably been stationed here in case an incident like this broke out.

"Phew, that was really close," one senior holy knight said.

"This guy really is as insane as they say…," remarked another.

"Shido Jukurius, that attack clearly violated the rules of the Sword Master Festival," the third declared.

"Sorry, bud, but you're coming with us to the holy knight station," the last one said.

As one of the senior holy knights approached Shido with a pair of handcuffs, the four boards holding him in place began to freeze.

"Get these creepy things off of me!" Shido yelled in anger, smashing the barriers to pieces.

"N-no way!"

"That restraint was enhanced with high gravity four times over!"

Shido swung Vanargand at the bewildered senior holy knights. "I'll kill you if you get in my way."

""""" ………"""""

He cowed the holy knights with a glare, then turned back to the collapsed Rahm.

"Die already, you bastard…," he said, raising his blade without hesitation.

"Stop right there, Shido!"

A woman with a slightly accented voice shouted, and Shido froze.

"M-Madam…," he croaked.

The chairwoman of Ice King Academy, Ferris Dorhein, had made her way onto the stage. "*Haah*… Always taking things too far. You do know he'll really succumb if you hit him again, right?"

"B-but, this goddamn scum was insulting us!" Shido protested.

"Do you intend to disobey me, Shido?" Ferris asked with an expression of sadness.

"…Tch, fine." Shido finally backed off and made Vanargand vanish.

"S-seize him!"

As soon as Shido's murderous aura faded, more than ten senior holy knights rushed forward to arrest him.

"Hey, that hurts… Would it kill you to be a little gentler?!" he said without a hint of fear. His usual ornery attitude continued as the holy knights led him away.

Silence overcame the venue.

"Shido broke through the Soul Attire of four senior holy knights with brute strength alone. He could be a real problem for us down the road…," the president muttered.

"You can say that again. He's grown so much since summer training camp. He may not be on my elite level yet, but he's probably not far," Lilim said.

"Uh, I don't think you'd stand a chance, Lilim…," Tirith retorted.

"Excuse me?!" Lilim exclaimed.

Meanwhile, I was feeling worried about something, too.

"I wonder if Shido will be okay…" This was now the second time Shido had caused a disturbance on a major stage, the first time being at the Elite Five Holy Festival. *The announcer said earlier that he was suspended for a month, just like I was…* I wondered if he would receive a harsher punishment this time.

"He'll obviously be reprimanded, but there's no way they'll expel him," Shii asserted confidently. "He has the backing of Ferris, and more importantly, *she* has the backing of the famous Rize Dorhein. Nobody picks a fight with the Blood Fox. I'm sure he'll just receive a short suspension like last time."

"That's good to hear...," I responded, feeling relieved.

"W-well, that brawl threw us off schedule a bit... But let's resume the tournament and perform the lottery for the third match!" the announcer said enthusiastically to reengage the crowd, resuming the Sword Master Festival.

■

The other Elite Five Academies took care of business and advanced, and eight teams remained at the end of the round. With the Sword Master Festival's Elite Eight set to begin, Thousand Blade was once again the first name drawn.

"Hoo..." I exhaled deeply. We were finally up. Since Snowfall Academy had withdrawn in the first round, this was Thousand Blade's first match of the knockout stage. *It's time to put everything I've learned to good use!* I thought, balling my fists.

"Hee-hee, I'm feeling a little nervous!" the president said.

"Who wants a piece of us? Give us your worst!" shouted Lilim.

"I'd rather avoid the Elite Five Academies, luck willing...," muttered Tirith.

Seeing how nervous even my upperclassmen were made me feel restless.

"Now then, which academy will vie with Thousand Blade Academy for a place in the semifinals?!" The announcer reached a hand into a giant box with "Sword Master Festival" written on it in large letters. The seeding from the group stage was dropped in the Elite Eight, and the matchups were instead decided by luck of the draw. "Let's see... Look at that! It's another Elite Five Academy, White Lily Girls Academy!"

Here it is! A fight against an Elite Five Academy other than Ice King! I thought, my competitive spirit flaring.

"W-we're done for...," Shii lamented.

"Th-this might be kinda tough...," Lilim admitted.

"This is clearly the end of the road for us...," Tirith said.

My teammates all hopelessly slumped their shoulders. Even the ever-positive Lilim's smile seemed forced.

"A-are they really that good?" I asked.

The president nodded emphatically. "They're better than good. White Lily has finished as the runner-up in five straight Sword Master Festivals. They've been utterly *dominant*," she explained.

"And this year they've added the best first year in the country. Her name is Idora Luksmaria. Everyone calls her the Wonder Child... Don't die on us, Allen!" Lilim added.

"Just do your best not to get killed...," Tirith said gravely.

The two girls actually seemed concerned for my safety. *She must be a really formidable opponent...,* I thought, astonished.

The announcer began her usual fighter introductions. "The first for Thousand Blade Academy is Allen Rodol! He doesn't belong to a school of swordcraft and he can't manifest his Soul Attire, but his overpowering strength and polished swordcraft are plain to see! He was undefeated and uninjured in Group A, making him something of a dark horse in this tournament!"

I walked onto the stage after she finished introducing me.

"YOU CAN DO IT, ALLEN!"

"KEEP YOUR COOL! WE'RE HERE FOR YOU!"

"YOU'RE REPRESENTING OUR CLASS, SO YOU'D BETTER WIN!"

I heard Lia's, Rose's, and Tessa's reassuring cheers from their seats in the crowd.

"Now for the first from White Lily Girls Academy. You all know her already—it's the Wonder Child, Idora Luksmaria! There's no need to give her a detailed introduction at this point, is there? Let's just sit back and admire the prowess of the girl hailed as the greatest first year in the country!"

A majestic swordswoman climbed onto the stage, and the crowd erupted into cheers.

"HEY, HEY, IT'S IDORA! SHE'S WHO I CAME HERE TO SEE!"

"AAAAAAH, I LOVE YOU IDORA! LOOK OVER HERE!"

Idora Luskmaria had beautiful, long, pure-white hair pulled back into a half-pony. She stood at about165 centimeters tall, above-average for a fifteen-year-old girl. Her eyes were a clear amber, her skin was white as snow, and her limbs were long and slender—she was a girl of truly unmatched beauty. She radiated dignity in the green-and-white dress of the White Lily uniform.

Man, she's a real crowd-pleaser... Idora was receiving thunderous applause from men and women alike. She stared at me fixedly on the other side of the stage without saying a word.

"Are you both ready?! The first duel starts—now!" the announcer declared for the entire venue to hear.

I drew my sword right on her signal and assumed the middle stance. *I'm facing Idora Luksmaria, the Wonder Child, the girl they say is the greatest first year in the country!* She was surely one of the strongest contenders I had faced thus far. *She's a more than satisfying opponent. Time to give her everything I have!*

And so my duel with Idora commenced.

■

Idora held her longsword in her right hand and shifted her weight slightly to the right. It was a bit of a unique stance.

You don't see a single-handed grip very often... Gripping your blade with both hands was better from an offensive and defensive perspective. The established practice in swordcraft today was to drop your center of gravity, keep your opponent in the center of your field of vision, and wrap both hands gently around the hilt of your sword

She deviated from that stance significantly. *But I can't let my guard down.* Idora was the crème de la crème of swordfighters. There must have been something to that unusual stance of hers.

I maintained the middle stance and examined her closely.

"...Ah," Idora said abruptly, as if just remembering something, before she sheathed her sword. Then, for some inexplicable reason, she walked toward me unarmed. "…Hmm." She halted in front of me as I held my stance, and stuck out her right hand.

"…What are you doing?" I asked, bewildered.

"A handshake… Do you not know what that is? It's a greeting where two people clasp hands," she deadpanned.

"I-I obviously know what a handshake is…" I definitely hadn't been expecting her to ask for a handshake after the duel already began. "I-it's nice to meet you," I stammered, taking her small hand in mine and exchanging a brief handshake.

"Yeah, same to you," she responded, before turning around and walking back to her original position, totally defenseless.

She's kind of weird… Her behavior was peculiar, almost like she lived in her own little world. *Would "airheaded" be the right way to describe her?* I wondered.

"Let's go," Idora said. She drew her sword and held it in her right hand, and once again assumed her unique stance with her weight shifted slightly to the right.

"Uh, I'm gonna start, okay?" I said. It was always important to make the first move. Waiting around was dangerous against a superior opponent. *I need to go on the attack and try to overpower her!*

I kicked off the ground and raced toward her, coming to a halt within striking range.

"Y-you're so fast!" she exclaimed.

Moving quickly to take advantage of her momentary stupor, I performed a downward diagonal slash toward her lightly defended left flank. "Ha!"

Yes, I've got her! I was positive I would deliver a clean hit, but instead, I heard the clang of metal on metal. "Huh?!"

"Not good enough," she said, blocking my attack with a *second sword* she drew with a reverse grip.

"A-a dual-blade style?!"

"Ha!"

Idora swung her right sword in a counterattack.

"…"

I dodged the attack fairly easily and jumped backward.

"...You are quite fast. Didn't think you'd make me pull my second blade so soon," she said, sliding her right foot up a half step and her left foot back a half step. She held her right hand slightly high and jerked her left behind her. It was a unique stance.

Her right hand is ready for a slash, and her left for a thrust... She's totally primed for offense.

I was taken off guard by the two blades. I had heard of the style before, but this was the first time I'd ever faced it. She had one more sword than I did, which inevitably gave her more options. *Looks like I'll have to go with my usual approach and try to overpower her.*

"...?!"

Just then, Idora got right in my face, interrupting my strategizing.

"Thunderclap Style—Heavy Thunder!"

She swung the two swords as fast as lightning, performing ten slash attacks.

"Ngh, Eighth Style—Eight-Span Crow!"

I tried to offset her attack with eight slashes of my own, but one of hers got through and grazed me on the left cheek.

"Nrgh...," I gasped.

At the exact same moment, one of my slashes from Eight-Span Crow landed on her right cheek.

"Gah...," she cried softly.

We had both inflicted mirroring wounds on the other's cheek. It was a total draw. *She has the obvious advantage when it comes to moves, but my two-handed grip has the advantage in strength.* That was what led to that result. She outnumbered my slashes by two, but Eight-Span Crow had greater power.

"You're so strong... Are you really human?" she muttered in disbelief, patting her cheek.

"Of course I am. I could say the same to you, Idora. Your speed is unreal," I responded.

"Ha-ha, thanks." She smiled kindly, then resumed her unique stance. I responded by firmly taking the middle stance.

"Now it's my turn!" I shouted.

"...Bring it on!" she answered.

The intensity of our duel picked up from there.

"Haaaaaaaa!"

I charged into range and attacked in rapid succession. Downward diagonal slashes, upward slices, downward flourishes, thrusts—Idora fought hard to fend off my great variety of moves.

It soon became clear that even had our single-hand and two-hand grips been reversed, I had a significant advantage in strength. Idora's stance grew more and more unsteady with each blow she blocked.

"Take that!" I yelled.

"Grrgh...," Idora grunted.

I slashed her in the side with a carefully aimed strike. Her face twisted in pain, and she took a large step forward in sync with the backswing of my sword.

"Thunderclap Style—Bolt from the Blue!"

As if seeking revenge for my blow, she began a series of lightning-quick slices.

Up, down, up, down, left, right, middle! I strained my eyes and successfully blocked the entire rush of seven consecutive slashes.

"You're kidding!" Idora was momentarily flustered; clearly, she had not expected me to block every single one of her attacks.

This is my chance! Seizing the moment, I launched into a move of my own.

"Cherry Blossom Blade Secret Technique—Mirror Sakura Slash!"

"Ngh..."

Rather than trying to counter my approaching eight slashes, she elected to leap backward. I had predicted she would do that. "First Style—Flying Shadow!" I timed a projectile slash to reach her the moment she landed.

"Crap," she grunted, and managed to block the blow despite her unstable posture. My true attack was yet to come, however.

"Fifth Style—"

"What, when did you—?!"

I had hidden behind Flying Shadow to quickly reach point-blank range, and then start to put all of my might into an attack.

"—World Render!"

"What the?!"

Idora began to take a defensive position, but then seemed to sense that she couldn't block this attack. She quickly jumped to the right to just barely evade it. Unfortunately for her, I was ready for that as well.

"Second Style—Hazy Moon!"

"Wha—gaaah!"

Two hidden slash attacks I had set during our duel grazed her on the left shoulder and her side. Red blood ran down her white skin.

...That was a good reaction. Idora had reflexively twisted her body the moment my Hazy Moons touched her, resulting in shallow wounds. They wouldn't hinder her ability to fight.

"Haah, haah..."

"..."

Idora had taken a few cuts, and I was still mostly untouched. It was fair to say the duel was going in my favor.

The announcer took advantage of our momentary pause to speak up. "I-I-I can't believe my eyes! Allen Rodol, a total unknown before this festival, is completely overpowering the Wonder Child! This swordsman is truly incredible! Who could have anticipated he'd possess this level of skill?!" she proclaimed loudly, trying to fire up the crowd. The crowd, however, remained dead quiet and watched our duel with bated breath.

"You're good, Allen. I mean that. I never would have imagined your skill with the blade would be superior to mine...," Idora muttered reluctantly, sheathing her two swords.

I knew exactly what was coming. *It's finally time...*

The air between us tensed, and an intimidating aura formed around her.

"You may be the best in our year when it comes to dueling without Soul Attire," she said.

"...I'll take that as a compliment," I responded, feeling somewhat embarrassed. No fight between elite swordfighters would ever occur without Soul Attire.

"I want to give you my all, Allen!" she declared. "Fulfill—Neba Grome!"

Two lances resembling blue flashes of lightning appeared out of thin air. *There it is... Her Soul Attire... The practically insurmountable barrier of talent that always stood in my way.*

The real battle started now. This was where the Wonder Child would unleash her full strength.

"Let's do this, Allen!"

"Give me your best shot!"

My desperate struggle against Idora was finally getting into gear.

■

Idora had finally manifested her Soul Attire, Neba Grome.

Everything until now was just a warmup. The real all-out duel begins now. I took a moment to psych myself up, and in the blink of an eye, she was gone. "Huh?!"

A second later, I heard a cold voice from behind.

"I'm right here."

"..."

I crouched reflexively, and Idora's horizontal sweep flashed overhead.

"Brace yourself," she said, transitioning right from her flourish into a fierce roundhouse kick. I spun around and crossed my arms to defend myself head-on, but it was to no avail.

"Whuh?!"

Her kick hit me with a violent impact that I couldn't believe came from those slender legs. *What is this strength?!* She sent me flying backward through the air, and I spun mid-flight to bring myself to a halt.

Idora calmly lowered the long right leg she used for the kick, and assumed her unique two-sword—or rather, two-lance—stance.

"...You've gotten even faster," I noted.

"Thanks. But I'm just getting started!" she responded. She let out a big breath, then yelled out, "Flying Thunder—Twenty Million Volts!"

Bluish-white light surged out of her body, filling the air with a crackling sound. *Is she charging her body with electricity?!* The strong electricity raced through her body and stimulated her cells. This technique must have improved her physical strength and reaction speed, enabling the inhuman movement she'd just displayed.

She can manipulate electricity... That's going to make this really difficult, I thought.

"Thirty Million Volts—Lightning Bolt!" Idora yelled, shooting violent, azure bolts of lightning straight at me from the rips of her lances.

"First Style—Flying Shadow!"

I sent a flying slash attack to meet it, but it vanished before the electricity. *Crap, Flying Shadow isn't good enough...* Seeing clearly that I wasn't going to match her attack's strength, I quickly dove to the left. I successfully dodged it, then looked up to find Idora standing right in front of me.

"Thunderclap Style—Bolt from the Blue!"

She inundated me with a turbulent, storm-like chain of slashes.

"Ngrh, haaaaah!"

Thrust, slash, horizontal sweep—I managed to block the first three strikes, but—*crap, they're too fast!*—blocking all of them was going to be impossible. I made a quick decision based on all of my sword fighting experience and leaped backward, fully aware that I would take a couple of hits.

The sharp tips of her lances cut through flesh on my side and my left leg.

"Grrgh..."

I did my best to bear the burning pain and dashed toward her as soon as I landed. "Haaaaaaa!"

My disadvantage will only grow if I stay on the defensive. I needed to get more aggressive to prevent her from attacking as she pleased.

"Eighth Style—Eight-Span Crow!"

"Thunderclap Style—Heavy Thunder!"

Our attacks cancelled each other out upon impact.

"Ooooooooh!"

"Haaaaaaaa!"

My sword screeched against the blades of her lances, sending sparks flying.

A problem was becoming clear. *She's too far away.* I couldn't get within striking range. Idora's lances had about twice the reach of my sword; it was hopeless trying to attack her from this distance. Her lances would strike me before my blade ever reached her.

Shoot... She was inflicting cut after cut. Feeling the need for a breather, I jumped back to put some distance between us.

"Fifty Million Volts—Thunderbird!"

A giant bolt of lightning transformed into a flock of small birds, which flew at me with tremendous speed. There were just over a hundred of them.

"Ngh, Eighth Style—Eight-Span Crow!"

I spread eight slash attacks in all directions to form a defensive barrier around myself. "Nggrgh?!" Unfortunately, the improvised shield was ineffective against a flock numbering over one hundred. After being struck by nearly every one of the electric attacks, I fell to my knees.

Th-this is really bad... I had never been electrocuted before. It was very different from the pain of being cut, burned, or hit with an explosion. The shock to my body was so great it threatened to knock me unconscious.

Idora didn't let a second go to waste while I was defenseless.

"Seventy Million Volts—White Whale!"

As if trying to end the duel right there, she released her strongest electric attack yet. The fulmination took the form of a giant whale with a bulging belly, and it moved toward me with its mouth wide open.

"F-Fifth Style—World Render!"

I sliced the whale apart using my strongest move, which could cut through space.

"Diffusion!"

"Huh?!"

Just then, the white whale expelled all of the electricity stored inside its body at once. White blanketed my vision, and I endured my most devastating shock yet.

"Ga-hah..."

Fighting desperately to cling to my fading consciousness, I braced my unsteady legs and somehow forced myself to stand. "Haah… Haah…" The air felt heavy. No matter how much I sucked in, it wouldn't seem to stay in my lungs. My situation looked hopeless, but I assumed the middle stance in spite of it all.

"Y-you're still standing…?" Idora's trembling voice echoed throughout the venue. "Most people would have died instantly after that attack. Even a powerful swordfighter would be put in a coma for a month if I hit them with it… Are you sure you're human, Allen?"

"Haah, haah… Trust me… It hurts…a lot…" I responded.

I had never taken such a powerful blow. My body was in rough shape, and I was only able to stand after mustering every last drop of willpower I had.

"…Huh. Your greatest asset seems to be that monstrous mental fortitude of yours. Unfortunately for you, however, this is the end of the road," Idora said, thrusting an azure lance at me. "Your inability to manifest your Soul Attire gives you no shot in this duel. You'll only be punishing yourself by continuing to fight. Just quit now."

Idora casually recommended that I surrender.

"You're right that I can't manifest my Soul Attire. I must look like an amateur to you, with your full mastery of Neba Grome," I began, sinking deeper and deeper into my consciousness as I talked—into the depths of my soul. "But there's still one thing I can do."

"What could you possibly do in that condition?" she asked, and immediately disappeared from my view. "You're done." I heard her voice behind me along with the sound of metal slicing through the wind. She was surely trying to end the bout.

I didn't have the strength to turn around, let alone avoid the attack. I did, however, have an ace up my sleeve. *If I use* this *with all my strength, my Sword Master Festival will undoubtedly come to an end.* My body wasn't yet strong enough to bear the brunt of its activation. This would knock me out for a day at least. *President, Lilim, Tirith…I leave the rest to you.*

Not even glancing at Idora's incoming strike from behind my back, I poured all the spirit power I had into the depths of my soul.

"Haaaaa*hrraaagh!*"

Darkness of a greater scale than ever before flowed out of my body.

"What the heck?!" Idora widened her eyes with shock and jumped back in retreat.

The pitch-black darkness enveloped me like armor. Strangely, the agony pulsing through my body quickly abated. This darkness apparently had healing powers as well.

"No way, is that your Soul Attire?!" she asked in disbelief, but I was already gone.

"I'm right behind you."

"Huh?!"

I circled around Idora in a flash and performed a horizontal sweep. She crouched reflexively and managed to dodge it.

"This is gonna hurt a bit," I announced, and followed my sweep with a roundhouse kick covered by darkness.

Idora turned around and crossed her arms, attempting to defend herself against my blow.

"What the?!"

However, my darkness-enhanced attack easily shattered her defense and sent her bouncing across the stage. *Wh-what...? Defending against his attack did nothing?!* she thought. Unable to slow her momentum after the great impact of my strike, she crashed into the wall of the venue.

Normally, an injury like that would be enough to knock someone out, but Idora stood up calmly. Though blood was running down her forehead, and her shoulders were heaving, her fighting spirit hadn't been diminished in the slightest.

"Haah, haah... What in the world is that strength?!" she inquired.

"Hmm... If I had to guess, this darkness might be a failed attempt at realizing my Soul Attire?" I answered. The darkness was only that—darkness. It was still far from the black sword, and I still had a long road of training ahead of me. *But I'm definitely getting closer!* It felt wonderful to have proof of that.

"How about we settle this, Idora," I said.

"Ah-ha-ha. To think you can still fight... You're the best, Allen Rodol!" she responded.

I assumed the middle stance, and she took her unique two-lance stance. Our eyes met, and she made the first move.

"Flying Thunder—Fifty Million Volts!"

The bluish-white electricity surrounding her body swelled, and her injuries began to quickly heal. The rapid stimulation of her cells seemed to enhance her self-healing.

"That's a truly amazing Soul Attire…," I observed.

"Ha-ha, you haven't seen anything yet!" she exclaimed, fully healed just a moment later. "Fifty Million Volts—Thunderbird!"

She swung one of her lances and sent over one hundred electric birds at me. This was the kind of multistage, long-distance attack I struggled with, but I wasn't concerned.

"That won't work anymore," I said as the birds all vanished the moment they touched my darkness. This substance had defended me against a punch from *him*; its power clearly surpassed Idora's electricity.

"Huh?!" she shouted.

Taking advantage of her brief moment of discomposure, I closed the distance between us with a single step.

"Eighth Style—Eight-Span Crow!"

"Ngh, Thunderclap Style—Heavy Thunder!"

My eight slashes met her ten.

"Waah?!"

My eight slices overcame her Heavy Thunder and inflicted sharp wounds on Idora's shoulder and thigh. Her eyes narrowed from the pain, and she leaped back to try to regain her composure. Not wanting to give her a chance to rest, I rushed forward.

"*Hraagh!*"

I brought my sword crashing down from above without hesitation.

"Grr…"

Idora crossed her lances and just barely blocked the attack. Our weapons locked, sending sparks flying. We both pushed, now engaged in a pure contest of strength.

"Oooooooorrrgh!"

"Haaaaaaaaaaa!"

We both screamed.

"*Hrragh!*"

"What?!"

I overpowered Idora and sent her flying backward through the air. She regained her balance mid-flight and landed nimbly on the stage.

"Not even Fifty Million Volts was strong enough... Do you have a self-strengthening Soul Attire?" Idora asked, biting her lower lip vexedly.

"Ah-ha-ha... Unfortunately, I don't know that yet," I answered. There was no way to know what kind of power my Soul Attire had until I manifested it.

"Continuing to fight is going to take a major physical toll on me. But I'll stop at nothing to defeat you!" Idora opened her eyes wide and got ready to fill her body with an electric current of even higher voltage. "Flying Thunder—Seventy Million Volts!" Her beautiful white hair stood up on end, and she held her grand azure lances up to the sky. "This should do it! Seventy Million Volts—White Whale!"

She created another giant white whale with a belly that bulged from the massive amount of electricity stored in its abdomen. I sliced at it without hesitation.

"Fifth Style—World Render!"

Idora smiled triumphantly. "You're done—Diffusion!" Lightning significantly more brutal than before enveloped my entire body.

"Ngh?!"

The violent crackling sound of the electricity ravaged my eardrums, and my vision was painted white. Her attack burned the stage black, and a peculiar, offensive smell filled the air.

"Haah, haah... Come on... Tell me your darkness is gone!" Idora's expression changed from hope to astonishment, then from astonishment to despair. "No way..."

I was surrounded by a cloak of darkness and totally uninjured.

"That tingled a little, but I guess I managed to block it," I said.

"Y-you monster...," she uttered, dumbfounded, leaving herself defenseless.

Thinking it would be cheap of me to just attack her in that state, I gave her a warning: "Now it's my turn."

"..."

I dropped my center of gravity and concentrated strength into my legs when—*Oh no...*—my vision suddenly wavered and the darkness surrounding my body fell into disarray. *Crap, I'm already out of time?!* This was the first time I had ever produced this much of the darkness, and I had been unaware of how long I would be able to maintain it.

"Hang on... Do you not have full control of that power yet?" Idora asked.

"Yeah, embarrassingly enough," I answered. It had only been two weeks since I'd manifested the darkness. I had learned how to manipulate it a little, but I hadn't gained full control over it yet.

"Hmm. That means I still have a chance!" Idora proclaimed, lifting her two lances toward the heavens. Right then, a huge bolt of lightning shot down from the cloudless sky into the tips of her spears.

"Huh?!" I gasped.

Idora ignored my astonishment and spoke calmly. "As far as I can tell, you can only control your darkness for a limited amount of time. I'm gonna force it out of you until your spirit power runs totally dry!" She readied her brilliantly shining lances and smiled boldly. "Let's do this, Allen!"

"Bring it!"

She wasted no time.

"One Hundred Million Volts—Imperata Grome!"

She sent a spiraling azure lightning strike at me with incredible speed. I responded by concentrating the pitch-black darkness into the tip of my sword to create a mock black sword.

"Sixth Style—Dark Boom!"

My darkness-enveloped projectile tore apart the stone stage, and our two all-out attacks collided ferociously.

"Haaaaaaaaa!"

"Oooooooooh!"

The lightning and the darkness raged violently, birthing an enormous shock wave. A moment later, her lightning strike and my Dark Boom vanished simultaneously.

Th-they canceled each other out?!

Th-they were equal in power?!

We both fell to our knees after performing our most powerful attacks. ""Haah, haah...""

I struggled to suck oxygen into my lungs and stay conscious. The darkness around my body was gone; that Dark Boom must have used up the last of my spirit power. *That's okay. Idora should be on her last legs, too!* I looked up to see how she was doing.

"Flying Thunder—Maximum One Hundred Million Volts!"

Idora literally transformed into blue lightning and calmly rose to her feet. *She still has this much fight left in her?!* Her appearance was so divine it took my breath away.

Idora joined her two lances in front of her chest. "Grome Alchemia," she muttered, melting the lances with violent lightning and merging them into one large sword. "Thunderblade—Indra!"

The sword was pure white from the blade to the handle to the guard, and it projected an overwhelming pressure. Idora held it in front of her navel in the middle stance.

I was out of spirit power, I had lost the darkness, and I was wounded all over. My situation was hopeless. And yet, a strange emotion surged within my heart.

Ha, ha-ha, ha-ha-ha!

I was having an absolute blast. It was fun exhausting my strength to the very last drop. It was fun fighting an opponent who appeared unbeatable. It was fun fighting with my life on the line.

Man... Dueling is a blast!

I felt a sudden throb of pain. My soul—actually, no. My blood, my flesh, my bones, and my entire body pulsed.

"...?!"

Next, I got a feeling like the *something* that had been blocking my way all this time *wavered*, and a *path* opened before me.

"What the...?!"

An unprecedented amount of darkness flowed out of the depths of my body. It showed no signs of stopping as it covered the entire stage in black.

I slowly got to my feet and assumed the middle stance.

"..."

"..."

It was quiet. We no longer had any need for words. After a moment of silence that could've lasted a second, a minute, or an hour for all I knew, we rushed at each other simultaneously.

"Ooooooooorgh!"

"Haaaaaaaaaaa!"

My jet-black darkness and her blue lightning met in the center of the stage.

"Gah..."

I sustained a slice to the chest, and it burned with pain. *That's a deep cut... It was going to be difficult to fight through this agony. But I have to hang on... I can't collapse yet!* Fighting hard to quell my rising blood, I grit my teeth and clung to consciousness by a thread.

I heard the sound of rustling clothes behind me. *Crap, Idora can still fight...* I roused myself to turn around with what little strength I had left, gripped my sword in my quivering hands, and forced myself into the middle stance.

"You win...Allen Rodol..."

Idora's Thunderblade Indra broke into two pieces, and she collapsed slowly forward onto the stage.

"I-Idora Luksmaria has fainted! Allen Rodol is the winner!"

The announcer's voice reverberated throughout the silent venue. The crowd immediately erupted into cheer.

"O-oh my god, what a fight! You're tellin' me they're both first years?!"

"Allen Rodol... How did a swordsman as brilliant as him remain unknown for so long?"

"The Wonder Child just lost! Th-this calls for an extra edition! Write the article now!"

I lifted my right hand to the crowd in response to their thunderous applause. That was how I achieved a spectacular victory over Idora Luksmaria in a serious duel where we both gave our absolute all.

■

After achieving victory in the firsts' battle, I dragged my fatigued body off the stage.

"That was incredible, Allen! I'm stunned you were able to defeat the Wonder Child!" the president exclaimed.

"You're not half bad! I can't believe I'm saying this, but I think you're as skilled as I am now!" added Lilim.

"Lilim, he's clearly better than all of us…," Tirith retorted.

My teammates raced toward me excitedly.

"Ah-ha-ha, thank you. It was a tough fight, but I pulled it off in the end."

Shii put her hand to her mouth as if just remembering something. "Ah, sorry. Treating your injuries should be top priority!" she said, beginning to walk to the doctor's office.

"Hold on, I don't think that's necessary," Lilim pointed out. "See, look at his body. His wound is already closing."

"""Huh?""" Shii, Tirith, and I responded simultaneously.

"Don't be ridicu… What the heck?!" the president shouted.

"It's almost completely healed already!" Tirith exclaimed.

"W-wow, it really is…," I said.

The deep gash on my chest had almost completely closed up. The bleeding had stopped, and the injury already looked a few days old.

"A-Allen, are you really human?" the president asked hesitatingly.

"There's no way a human would be capable of this strength and recovery rate," Lilim said.

"This would actually be easier to accept if you told us you're *not* human…," Tirith added.

"Ah-ha-ha, enough with the jokes. I'm clearly just an ordinary person," I answered with an awkward smile.

"Hmm… On a different note, you really do have a nice body," Shii said admiringly.

"Let's see… Wow, you're right, Shii. His muscles are so elastic. All your training has really paid off, Allen!" Lilim agreed.

"Your skin feels so nice…," Tirith praised.

All three of them ran their thin fingers across my chest and abs.

"H-hey, come on… Th-that tickles!" I protested, fighting to prevent myself from laughing.

"Attention all! Now that the spectacular first duel is in the books, it's time to move on to the duel between both academy's seconds!" the announcer said, resuming the tournament. Still excited from the last match, the audience began to roar.

I'd noticed earlier that Idora was laid on a stretcher and carried to the doctor's office to have her serious injuries treated. She was talking to the medical officials, so it didn't look like her life was in danger.

"All right, it's my turn! I'm not gonna let this incredible momentum you've built for us go to waste!" Lilim announced.

"Good luck, Lilim!" I encouraged.

"You'd better not lose!" warned the president.

"I hope you know how important this duel is...," added Tirith.

"Ha, don't worry! I got this!"

She gave us a thumbs-up, and walked to the stage for her duel in high spirits.

■

Unfortunately, Lilim and Tirith both lost their duels. White Lily Girls Academy boasted an impressive talent pool, and the swordswomen entrusted with the second and third positions were incredibly skilled.

The vice-captain's duel was next. Shii achieved victory with a brilliant performance that lived up to her name as an Arkstoria. The score was now 2-2 as the match carried on to the captain's duel, but that presented us with a problem.

Haah, I guess this is it... Our captain—the vice president of the Student Council, Sebas Chandler—wasn't here. He had been missing ever since he'd traveled to the Holy Ronelian Empire. His absence had meant we needed to secure the victory before the match reached the captain's duel, so unfortunately, our hands were now tied.

"All right, everybody—it's time for the captain's duel between Thousand Blade Academy and White Lily Girls Academy!" the announcer declared before moving on to her usual fighter introductions. "The captain of Thousand Blade is Sebas Chandler! According to my notes, Sebas is the *vice* president of Thousand Blade's Student Council, one rank below Student Council President Shii Arkstoria! Despite that, Sebas is said to be the superior swordsman!"

The announcer finished reading Sebas's introduction, but no one climbed to the stage. An awkward silence descended upon the venue.

"...Huh? S-Sebas Chandler! Please take the stage!" the announcer called out once more, but her voice echoed unanswered.

"He's not showing up, President," I said.

We held out as long as we could for the miniscule chance that Sebas would return in time for the captain's duel, but unsurprisingly, he wasn't going to show.

"Haah, oh well. We have to withdraw," Shii responded.

Just as she was about to speak to the Sword Master Festival Executive Committee on our behalf, a small jet passed overhead. Someone seemed to emerge from it.

"Huh... AAAAARRRGGGHHH?!"

It was a boy in ragged clothing, plummeting at tremendous velocity. *He threw himself out?! There's no way he's gonna survive from that height!* His fall speed quickly increased as gravity pulled him down. Less than a second later...

"GAAAH!"

...The strange boy crashed into the center of the stone stage, forming a large crater around him. The crowd was shocked into silence.

"...Phew, that was a close one. *Great* time for my parachute to fail. I could've really gotten hurt there...," the boy said, standing up casually and brushing dust off his clothes.

Wh-who is this guy?! He was unhurt after falling hundreds of meters. This incredible feat reminded me of when Chairwoman Reia and Eighteen had jumped out of a helicopter during summer training camp.

I then noticed something as I observed him. *Th-that black overcoat... Is he a member of the Black Organization?!* He was wearing the signature black garb of the group. *Crap, is he after Lia?!* I thought, starting to draw my sword.

"S-Sebas?! What in the world are you doing falling from the sky?!" the president shouted, her eyes wide with surprise.

"What took you so long, Sebas? I thought you might've died!" Lilim exclaimed.

"You can't just go missing for months like that...," Tirith chastised.

Lilim and Tirith both looked as if they thought of him as a close friend.

Th-this guy is Vice President Sebas?!

Sebas Chandler had wavy brown hair, and a kind, easygoing persona. He was about the same height as me, and strangely, he was dressed as a member of the Black Organization.

"Man, how lucky am I! What are the odds I would land next to my beloved president... Is this fate?!"

He rushed to kneel before Shii without even looking at Lilim and Tirith. He seemed peculiar.

"You're late! What in the world have you been doing all this time?!" the president asked, sounding like an angry older sister.

"S-sorry about that... Sneaking into the Holy Ronelian Empire was surprisingly easy, but getting back took forever. I couldn't find a blood diamond for the life of me, and to make matters worse, I had to spend the whole time running from a bunch of weaklings wearing these black clothes. I am unworthy as your knight...," Sebas said, clenching his teeth and punching the stage in frustration. It looked to me like he was in love with the president.

"Okay, I understand what took you so long. But don't call yourself my knight, okay?" Shii, however, didn't seem to return his feelings at all. Sebas's passion was entirely unanswered. "So...did you find one?" she asked.

"Why, of course! They're all yours. These are blood diamonds, famed for their rarity and only found deep underground in the Holy Ronelian Empire!" Sebas declared, producing two fist-sized crystals from his pocket.

He actually found some blood diamonds?! I thought with astonishment.

Shii's face lit up with a wide smile. "Wow, they're beautiful! Thank you, Sebas!"

"I-it was nothing, my love!" Sebas responded, looking genuinely happy to have received her thanks.

She clearly has him wrapped around her little finger, but I guess it's fine if he doesn't mind...

"Well, it's your turn, Sebas! Go defeat White Lily's captain!" the president ordered. She sure did ask a lot of him.

"My turn? I don't know what you mean, but your wish is my command! Consider this 'captain' toast!" Sebas responded, proudly drawing the blade at his hip.

W-wow, that doesn't look good... You could tell how rusty his sword was from a distance. It definitely didn't look like it was in good enough shape to use in the Sword Master Festival.

"Wh-what a sensational entrance that was! Has anyone in the history of this festival ever taken the stage in such an eye-catching manner?!" the announcer proclaimed, obviously having no idea of the circumstances behind Sebas's appearance. The crowd went wild in response. They thought his entrance was a performance.

"Facing the crowd-pleasing Sebas Chandler is the captain of White Lily Girls Academy—Lily Gonzales! She practices the Vajra School of Swordcraft, which is famed for its overwhelming strength! She may also boast the greatest physical strength of her generation! She's an inspiration to women everywhere!"

A female student walked onto the stage following that introduction. *Sh-she's huge!*

Lily Gonzales was built like a bear, slightly smaller than Ms. Paula, but still enormous. Her blond hair was cut short, and she had a tough, chiseled face. A strong confidence was visible in her clear eyes. She had well-toned muscles and an imposing posture, and I could tell at a glance what a tremendously skilled swordswoman she was.

"Are you both ready?! On my mark—begin!" the announcer proclaimed.

Lily wasted no time in summoning her Soul Attire after the announcer's signal.

"Bludgeon—Void Collision!"

A giant sword over two meters long appeared from a rift in midair. She grabbed it and leaped to action.

"Vajra Style—Boulder Smash!"

Lily approached Sebas with one giant step, lifted her blade overhead, and swung it down with terrific strength. However, her move didn't go according to plan.

"You're too slow."

In the blink of an eye, her Soul Attire was smashed to pieces.

"I-impossible...," Lily uttered, collapsing face-forward onto the stage.

H-he's so fast!

Sebas's slashes were too fast for the eye to follow. *Did he just swing his sword over thirty times?!* Not only were his lightning-quick slash attacks strong enough to destroy her Soul Attire, they'd even knocked her unconscious.

He's good. He probably surpassed the president in terms of pure skill with the blade.

"L-Lily Gonzales has been knocked out! Sebas Chandler is the winner!" the announcer declared loudly, and the venue buzzed at the shocking outcome.

Sebas made his way back to us after the duel. "So, President, who the heck is this guy? He looks like a Thousand Blade Student, but...," he asked, eyeing my uniform.

"Wow, it's rare for you to take an interest in other people. Can I ask why he caught your eye?" Shii responded.

"How could he not? It's not every day you see an inhuman monstrosity of his outstanding caliber wearing our uniform. Just where did you find him? He's like a giant mass of power. I doubt there are many who could beat this beast...," Sebas said with a meek expression, fear and caution visible in his eyes.

Inhuman monstrosity? Beast? That was a horrible way to speak about someone who hadn't even had a chance to introduce themselves yet.

■

Despite Sebas's cruel words, I decided to go ahead and introduce myself to him.

"Um... You're Sebas Chandler, right? It's nice to meet you, I'm—" I started, but was interrupted.

"Thousand Blade Academy is the winner of this spectacular show-down between two Elite Five Academies! Are the glory days of Thousand Blade finally back?" the announcer declared loudly.

"I didn't think they had a chance against White Lily. This is a brand-new Thousand Blade!"

"Allen Rodol, Shii Arkstoria, Sebas Chandler... Those are names worth remembering!"

"Especially that first year with the darkness! Who could've seen him beating the Wonder Child?!"

Deafening cheers and generous praise rained down upon us from the audience.

"Hmm-hmm-hmm, do you hear that? We're amazing!" Lilim said, puffing out her chest with pride.

"Uh, Lilim... We both lost, remember...," Tirith jabbed.

That was so like them I couldn't help but chuckle.

"We've got you now, Sebas Chandler!" a deep voice suddenly called out, and over thirty senior holy knights rushed into the venue.

"Don't move!"

"Sebas Chandler, you are under suspicion for multiple charges of assault. You're coming with us to the holy knight station!"

"You'll regret it if you resist!"

They had all already manifested their Soul Attire, and they looked ready to strike at the first wrong move. Confusion spread through the crowd at the sudden development.

"Haah, you guys don't know when to quit...," Sebas said, shrugging in annoyance. He seemed to know why the holy knights were there.

"Oh my god, Sebas, what did you do this time?" the president asked in exasperation, not sounding particularly surprised.

"Well, you see, the border defense had been crazy fortified when I got back, so I had no choice but to get a little physical. I couldn't exactly tell them where I'd been...," he answered.

Liengard had placed a travel ban on the Holy Ronelian Empire. There was no way the border patrol would have authorized a trip with a purpose as silly as finding a blood diamond for a punishment game.

He was really unlucky, though... It was only recently that the border defense had been fortified. House Arkstoria had strengthened the country's defenses because Zach Bombard and Tor Sammons, two very dangerous individuals, had slipped through.

"Good lord... Sebas, please go with the holy knights before this develops into a bigger problem. I'll send someone to get you later, so cooperate until then, okay?" Shii instructed.

"Sure thing, President! Hey, you all had better thank this fine young lady. It's her mercy that saved you all from getting a beatdown!" Sebas boasted to the large crowd of senior holy knights.

Man, he sure has guts... He was clearly convinced he could defeat the entire group of them.

Shii raised her eyebrows. "Sebas? I told you to cooperate."

"S-sorry about that!" Sebas followed her orders and allowed the senior holy knights to take him away.

What exactly is their relationship? I decided I would ask her about it once things calmed down.

Triumphant in our great victory over White Lily Girls Academy, we returned to Thousand Blade's assigned spectator seating.

"Phew...," I said, sitting down and allowing my body to relax.

"Hey, Allen. Do you think you can manage another fight?" Shii asked hesitatingly.

"Hmm... I should be fine as long as my next opponent isn't as strong as Idora," I answered. I thought I had exhausted all of my spirit power in my fight against her, but for some reason, I couldn't have felt better. The cut on my chest had already closed completely, and I felt fit to burst with a strange kind of energy.

What in the world is this? I had a strange feeling like there was *something other* than spirit power traveling through my body. This wasn't the first time this had happened; I experienced the exact same feeling on one prior occasion. *I'm pretty sure it was during my duel with the president during the Club Budget War...*

"H-huh. You can still fight after all that...," the president responded with a stiff smile. "What about you two, Lilim and Tirith?"

"Uh, well... Sorry. I don't know if I can manage," Lilim admitted.

"Sorry, I'm all out of spirit power," Tirith answered.

They both shook their heads in embarrassment.

"I feel the same way. I really gave my all during that last vice-captain duel. I don't even have the strength to summon my Soul Attire," Shii said.

Shii, Lilim, and Tirith were all completely exhausted, and Sebas was absent since he'd been taken away by the senior holy knights. This looked like the end of the road.

"I don't want to, but we have no choice but to withdraw." The president sighed, coming to a decision.

"Yeah, you're right...," I agreed.

It was a shame, but there was nothing we could do about it. Duels between swordsmen were all-out affairs. The girls would risk serious injury if they forced themselves to fight while worn out like this. The best thing to do was to quit now and then rest up to wait for our next opportunity.

"I'm sorry, Allen. Your upperclassmen shouldn't hold you back like this."

"Sorry, Allen. It's not often I feel like I didn't train hard enough."

"I feel really guilty..."

My teammates apologized to me in turn, each bowing their head.

"D-don't worry about it! I'm feeling a little tired too now that I think about it, so this works for me," I said, telling them a white lie to avoid hurting their feelings and bring the conversation to a close.

■

Our withdrawal in the semifinals gave us a fourth-place finish. I regretted that we were unable to participate in the championship match on the final day, but we received a standing ovation from the crowd for our upset over White Lily Girls Academy.

I need to work even harder to ensure we reach the finals next year!

My normal school life was resuming tomorrow. *Ha-ha, between Soul Attire classes, strength training, and working on my control of the darkness, I'm gonna be really busy!* Having that many things to do meant that I could still get stronger. That thought put a smile on my face.

Thousand Blade's time at the Sword Master Festival came to an end after a long closing ceremony, and my upperclassmen in the audience raced toward me at the first opportunity.

"I watched every match, Allen! You were incredible! You were the only one to go undefeated!"

"Hey, let me join that Practice-Swing Club of yours! I want you to teach me swordcraft!"

"Wait, how do you have so much energy left?!"

Surrounded by my Thousand Blade friends, I started off for the National Crusade Coliseum's exit. Something caught my eye on the way.

Wh-what the heck?! I couldn't believe my eyes. Extra editions of a few different newspapers were being handed out by the exit. There was nothing strange about that, of course; the problem was that my face prominently decorated the front page of each tabloid.

Unknown Swordsman Allen Rodol Hands the Wonder Child a Shocking Defeat!

The Title of Strongest First Year Has Been Stolen! What is the Secret Behind Allen Rodol's Strength?

Allen Rodol is a Rising Star Surrounded by Darkness!

I could read the large font of the headlines from a distance.

What's going on here?! I froze like a statue, caught completely off guard.

"Wow, you've just become famous...," the president said.

"Man, I'm jealous! Just you watch—I'm gonna do so well next time that 'Lilim Chorine' will become a household name throughout the country!" Lilim proclaimed.

"Personally, I would find this really embarrassing...," Tirith muttered.

My teammates all politely took a copy of each.

Why did this have to happen...? No matter where I looked, it was impossible to avoid seeing my giant face being handed out. Everyone who'd received a copy glanced my way.

"L-let's get out of here..." I set off back to the academy at a breakneck pace, with my upperclassmen following behind me. After making my way through the winding streets of Aurest, I finally arrived at the dorm where Lia and I lived.

"Phew, I'm exhausted..." I sighed.

"Ah-ha-ha, I'll bet. That was kinda rough," Lia responded.

"Yeah, those newspapers really threw me for a loop."

I set my sword down in its usual place, then sank into the sofa and exhaled deeply.

"Haah..."

Strangely, I felt mentally exhausted but physically full of energy. I couldn't tell if I was feeling well or not. *The best thing to do at times like this is go to bed early.* Following my own advice, I ate dinner, took my bath, and got in bed with Lia.

"Good night, Lia."

"Good night, Allen."

I turned the light off and closed my eyes. Ten minutes passed, then twenty, then thirty. *Something's off, right? ...Yeah, definitely.* There was something I couldn't stop thinking about, and I was unable to fall asleep.

"Hey, Lia. Are you awake?" I asked.

"...Yeah. What's up?" she responded from her spot next to me in bed.

"Um, well... Sorry if this is just a misunderstanding, but you've been looking kind of down."

Lia had been acting strangely since the end of the Sword Master Festival. She was smiling like she always did, but every now and then it seemed like a shadow passed over her face.

"...Yeah, just a little," she answered, sinking restlessly beneath the covers.

"Do you want to try talking about whatever's bothering you? 'You'd be surprised by how much better you'll feel after confiding in someone,'" I suggested. That was something I'd once heard from the Time Hermit, who proved to be a great listener.

"I guess I can try... I first got this feeling when you defeated Idora in that amazing duel. The entire crowd cheered for you and our upperclassmen praised you so proudly... That made me really happy. But it

also felt like you had gone to some distant place out of my reach… I feel this tightness in my chest whenever I think about that. What is this sensation? I don't really understand…," Lia murmured hesitatingly before finally falling silent.

"Really…"

"…Yeah."

"…"

"…"

An awkward silence fell between us.

A tightness in her chest… I'm really not sure what that means. Unfortunately, I had no knowledge of psychiatry. I wasn't qualified to determine what was causing the pain in Lia's chest.

"I don't know what it is that you're feeling, Lia. But I can say one thing for sure."

"…What's that?"

"I'll never leave your side. I'm not going anywhere without you. We're going to be together forever."

"…Really?"

Lia poked her head half above the covers and stared at me intently.

"Yeah, it's a promise," I answered affirmatively.

"Th-thanks…"

She once again slid under the covers and fell silent.

"…Do you feel a little better after talking about it?" I asked.

"Yeah, I feel really…happy," she responded.

"That's good to hear."

I grabbed Lia's hand, and we fell asleep together.

CHAPTER 2

Top Secrets & The Thousand Blade Festival

The days passed quickly after the excitement of the Sword Master Festival. It was now the beginning of September, and the intense heat of summer was giving way to the cooler weather of fall.

Having finished morning classes, Lia, Rose, and I headed for the Student Council room with lunches in hand.

"It's been getting cool out lately," I said, looking out a window and making small talk.

"Yeah. I really like the weather at this time of year," Lia responded.

"Hmm, I like it a little cooler than this, personally," Rose shared.

They both looked to me as if asking for my opinion.

"Let me think… I like fall a lot because swinging my sword in the cool weather is refreshing," I answered.

"What do you think of winter?" Lia posited.

"Oh, winter is good, too. The cold inspires me to really concentrate on each swing."

"How do you feel about spring?" asked Rose.

"Hmm, I like spring, too. Practicing my swings outside in the warm weather is really comfortable."

""And what about summer?"" they asked together.

"Summer is nice, too. I really love the intense heat. It's so rewarding to push myself to train in that environment."

"Ha-ha, you judge all of them by how it feels to train," Lia laughed.

"You've always been a fitness freak," Rose said.

"H-have I...?" I responded questioningly before realizing that we had made it to the Student Council room. I knocked three times, and a voice called for us to enter.

"Good morning, President," I said.

"Morning, Allen, Lia, and Rose," the president responded with a gentle smile. She had gotten to the room before us.

Lilim and Tirith waved at us from where they sat on the sofa further in.

"Now that we're all here, let's get our regular meeting started!" the president announced, clapping her hands and starting our "meeting."

We ate lunch and made conversation just like we always did—it was a fun time. According to Shii, Sebas was still in custody under suspicions of being connected to the Black Organization because he was wearing their black garb. It sounded like it was going to take a little longer for him to return to Thousand Blade.

"By the way, it's almost time for the Thousand Blade Festival. Has your class decided what it's going to do, Allen?" the president asked, broaching a new topic.

""""...Thousand Blade Festival?""""

Lia, Rose, and I all answered in confusion.

"Oh, have you not heard of it? The Thousand Blade Festival is an annual event held at this academy! It's basically a cultural festival!" Lilim explained cheerfully.

"Lots of guests come from all over to see it every year. It's always a big success...," Tirith added.

A school festival... I hadn't had any friends at Grand Swordcraft Academy, so this would be my first opportunity to enjoy an event like this.

"Judging from that reaction, I'm guessing you haven't decided on your event yet. I'm sure you'll hear about it in homeroom soon," Shii said with a bright smile. It looked like she was really looking forward to the festival.

"Has your class already decided what it's doing?" I asked.

"Naturally. The students of Class 2-A are...," the president began.

"...Using three classrooms to make a jumbo-sized haunted house!" finished Lilim.

"I'm the director, by the way. I'm very good at haunted houses...," Tirith noted.

The three of them struck spooky poses in perfect sync.

"You will come see it, right?" the president asked with an ominous grin.

"Yeah, of course," I replied cheerfully, but Lia and Rose didn't show the same enthusiasm.

"A-a haunted house? Those are for kids! We're way too old to waste time on something like that, r-r-right, Rose?"

"Y-yeah, Lia's right! N-n-no swordswoman worth her salt would waste time on a festival event like that when she could be devoting herself to her training!"

They both must have been scared of ghosts. The president picked up on that and smiled wickedly. "Oh, don't tell me... Are you two *scared*?"

""No way!"" Lia and Rose shouted, giving in to her obvious provocation.

"Great! I expect to see you there, then. Allen said he's coming, so you have no reason to refuse, right?"

""...""

They were totally trapped.

"Y-yeah, we'll be there!" Lia said.

"F-fine, I'll go to your silly haunted house!"

The trembling in their voices belied their false confidence.

...Are they gonna be okay? Lia and Rose were both visibly shaking. It was clear that they were bluffing.

"If you two are scared, you don't have to force yourselves—" I started, trying to give them an out.

"Wh-where'd you get that idea? I-I'm not afraid of ghosts!" Lia retorted.

"Y-yeah! Don't be rude, Allen!" Rose snapped.

They were both too stubborn to own up to their fear.

"Hmm-hmm, this is going to be fun! Just so you know, our class did a haunted house last year, too... It was so terrifying that over ten people fainted out of fright," Shii informed us.

"Mwa-ha-ha! They say that once you've entered our haunted house, you'll be too scared to even go to the bathroom alone at night!" Lilim boasted.

"I want to see everyone trembling with terror…!" Tirith said.

Lia and Rose stiffened and went pale in response to our upperclassmen's threats.

"" …""

If they scare easily, they should just say so…, I thought with a bitter smile.

"Hmm, are you okay with scary stuff, Allen?" the president asked.

"I'll bet you're really hard to scare. You look innocent enough, but I saw your true, wicked colors when you cheated at poker with Shii," Lilim said.

"I'd love to break through that calm persona of yours and see some real fear…," Tirith muttered ominously.

They all turned their attention to me.

"Ah-ha-ha, I don't think I'm necessarily difficult to scare, but… I'm just not afraid of ghosts," I answered. Sure, I'd had a few sleepless nights after hearing Ol' Bamboo's ghost stories when I lived in Goza Village, but I stopped believing in spirits around the time I entered middle school.

"Wow, you sound pretty confident."

"He's so calm. This is gonna be a real challenge…"

"I'll have to step up my game to break him…"

They all looked full of determination.

"…Oh, it's almost time to get back to class, President," I said after looking at my watch and seeing there were only five minutes left of our lunch break.

"Wow, time sure flies when you're having fun. See you tomorrow, Allen, Lia, and Rose," she responded.

Our meeting now over, we left the Student Council room and headed to our first afternoon class.

■

Once our afternoon lessons ended, we returned to homeroom.

"Phew, that was another exhausting day." I sighed.

"Yeah, my whole body aches," Lia grumbled.

"Chairwoman Reia's classes are really demanding," Rose said.

I passed the time by making casual conversation with Lia and Rose and getting my things ready to go until the classroom door flew open.

"Hello, boys and girls! Way to overcome another hard day of classes! I don't have anything to discuss for afternoon homeroom, so you're free to leave!" Chairwoman Reia said, bringing homeroom to a quick end. She then addressed me with a slightly stiff voice. "Allen, I want to speak with you. Please come to my office alone when you get the chance."

"...? Yes, ma'am," I responded.

"I'll be waiting for you."

She gave a satisfied nod and briskly left the classroom.

"Reia looked unusually serious," Lia noted.

"She told you to come alone, too... What does she want?" Rose wondered.

They both wore puzzled expressions.

"Well, I'm gonna go ahead and go," I said.

"Okay. We'll be training in the usual spot."

"Come as soon as you're done, all right?"

"Sure thing."

I parted from Lia and Rose and left the classroom. Many long hallways later, I arrived at the chairwoman's office. I cleared my throat and knocked on the black door.

"Enter," the chairwoman called out formally.

"Yes, ma'am," I responded, and opened the door to find the chairwoman sitting in her work chair with a troubled expression on her face.

What's going on? Did something bad happen? I thought before she spoke up.

"Thanks for coming, Allen. I have a few things I want to talk to you about, but first, congratulations on taking fourth place in the Sword Master Festival! Defeating White Lily Girls Academy and reaching the semifinals was a truly great accomplishment!" She congratulated me with a kind smile.

"Thank you. I only got as far as I did because of Shii, Lilim, and Tirith," I responded.

"It was certainly a team effort, but you don't need to be so humble. You went undefeated in the group stage and the knockout stage, giving you the best record in the entire tournament. You should have more confidence in yourself, and take pride in your performance," the chairwoman said, pausing briefly before continuing. "Now, on to what I called you here for... You've achieved nationwide recognition after defeating Idora Luksmaria."

"R-really?"

"Yeah, really. You are now undoubtedly the most popular first year in Liengard," she declared definitively. "That's why there's something I need to tell you."

Her expression was uncharacteristically grim.

"Wh-what is it?"

I gulped as I waited for her to continue. It took about two minutes.

"It's about the cursed 100-Million-Year Button."

I couldn't believe what I just heard. *I've never told anyone about the 100-Million-Year Button.* It sounded like something out of a fairy tale, so I didn't think anyone would believe me.

"H-how do you know about that?!"

"Because I pushed the button once myself."

"Y-you...what?!"

"Yeah, that's right. I once spent an eternity in the World of Time, just like you...," she muttered, staring off into the distance.

"Does that mean you've met the Time Hermit, too?" I asked.

"That annoying old geezer with the snow-white beard? Yeah, I know him," she answered.

"..."

There was no doubt about it. The chairwoman had pushed the 100-Million-Year Button after receiving it from the Time Hermit, just like me.

"S-so... What do you have to tell me about the 100-Million-Year Button?!" I asked, leaning forward in my chair.

"Hmm, before we get into it... Can you promise me that you won't repeat a word of this to anyone else?" Reia asked, looking directly into my eyes.

"Y-yes, ma'am. But why can't I tell anyone about it?" I inquired. I hadn't been planning to tell anyone about the button in the first place, but I couldn't help but be curious about why she would want me to swear to secrecy.

"Let's see, where should I begin," she said, crossing her arms anxiously. "I'll start by sharing what we've learned. Basically, the 100-Million-Year Button is a cursed object in the Time Hermit's possession. They are quite old—the existence of both the hermit and the button have been known for centuries."

"C-centuries?!"

"Yes, he has long surpassed a normal human lifespan. Given that he calls himself the Time Hermit, he could very well be immortal. He's closer to a spirit than a human."

A *spirit*... If memory served, the Time Hermit did give off a kind of inhuman vibe.

"I don't know what that old fart is trying to accomplish, but he spends his time wandering the world and handing the 100-Million-Year Button to special swordsmen who possess innate talent."

That didn't feel right to me based on what I remembered from my encounter with the Time Hermit.

"It's not often that word of the Time Hermit reaches the public. Actually, it's extremely rare. The reason for that is because most swordsmen commit suicide from being unable to withstand the 100-million-year hell."

"..."

That brought back some unpleasant memories.

"Those who overcome the curse of the 100-Million-Year Button and escape from the World of Time are called Transcendents," she continued.

"...Transcendents."

"Yep. And here's our problem—a large organization has been gathering Transcendents and operating in the shadows of society as of late."

"Is that the Black Organization?"

"That's right. You're quick on the uptake." The chairwoman nodded and took a sip of water from the glass on her desk. "You left quite a mark at the Sword Master Festival. A virtual unknown just defeated Idora Luksmaria, the Wonder Child; it's not every year you see something like that. As you know, the Sword Master Festival draws a lot of attention. There is no doubt that word of your prowess has reached the Black Organization."

She paused briefly.

"On top of that, you've already single-handedly defeated the famous Immolation Zach Bombard. Zach is a member of the Black Organization, and we can safely assume that your victory is common knowledge to them. So what I'm getting at is this—there is a high chance the Black Organization is going to reach out to you. They are going to try to recruit you."

"Wh-what? Did you say 'recruit'?"

"Yeah, it's a perfectly reasonable assumption. Stay on your guard, okay? Those criminals are nothing if not persistent, and they won't hesitate to use dirty tricks to achieve their goals."

"G-got it... I'll be careful."

"That's what I want to hear."

There was no way I would join the organization that kidnapped Lia, but I supposed it would be best to keep my guard up.

"In summary—the Black Organization is currently gathering Transcendents, and based on how they've acted so far, there is a high chance they are going to scout you. If anyone ever asks you about the 100-Million-Year Button, feign ignorance. I guarantee they will be a member of the Black Organization," the chairwoman warned.

"Y-yes, ma'am...," I responded with a nod.

"All right, that's all I have to tell you," Reia said, downing the glass of water.

"Thank you for taking the time to warn me about this," I said graciously.

"Don't worry about it. I'm this academy's chairwoman and your homeroom teacher, after all." She smiled, before changing the subject slightly. "By the way, I ask this out of pure curiosity... How long were you imprisoned in the World of Time, Allen?"

"Ummm, sorry. I don't remember exactly how many years it was," I admitted.

"You can give me a broad estimate."

"Okay... I'm pretty sure it was over a billion years."

I repeated the one-hundred-million-year training experience multiple times, and stopped counting somewhere after ten. I hadn't exactly been in the state of mind to keep track of things at the time.

"...Huh?" The chairwoman went still as a statue. "S-sorry, let me make sure I heard that right. Did you just say 'over a billion years'?"

"Yes, ma'am. I was in the World of Time for at least that long."

I was pretty sure I hadn't pressed the button twenty times, at least.

"Th-that's insane...!" she muttered hoarsely, her mouth hanging open. "H-how in the world did you fill that colossal amount of time?"

"Hmm... Mainly with practice swings, as I recall."

While I had spent some of that time developing a collection of skills, including Flying Shadow, Hazy Moon, Dark Boom, Eight-Span Crow, and more, I really had spent most of it swinging my sword.

"Y-you spent over a billion years just doing *practice swings*?!" she stammered.

"U-uhh, yeah...," I responded.

"Huh... You really are one of a kind," she muttered in disbelief, and sighed loudly. "*Haah*... Well, never mind. Forget I brought that up."

"O-okay..."

"I'll say this one more time—what we discussed here today is classified information known only to a select few. I'm counting on you to keep it to yourself, okay?" the chairwoman reminded me.

"Yes, ma'am."

"All right, that's all I have for you. Sorry for taking up so much of your time."

"No, I appreciate it. Thank you very much."

I excused myself and left the chairwoman's office.

I can't believe Chairwoman Reia pushed the 100-Million-Year Button,

too… It truly was a small world. I never would have imagined that a person who had been through the same strange experience was so close by.

She said the Black Organization might try to recruit me… There was no way I would join a group that had kidnapped Lia. *It's a massive criminal syndicate, though.* There was a good chance that refusing them would cause them to fly into a rage and attack me. Considering that, I needed to keep my guard up.

"All right… I guess I should go join up with Lia and Rose," I said to myself, and headed for the courtyard where the Practice-Swing Club met.

■

Allen left the room.

"Th-that's absurd… He spent over a billion years in solitude in that empty world?! I was ready to break down at five hundred years, and I pride myself on my mental toughness! How did his mind survive that?!"

Reia's question echoed unanswered in her spacious office.

The Time Hermit only called it the 100-Million-Year Button for show. Aside from Allen, no one had ever returned to the real world after living through the full one hundred million years. The prisoner always went insane and committed suicide if they were unable to destroy the World of Time before then. Even Reia would have lost her mind and met a tragic end if she hadn't smashed the World of Time to pieces with her fists in her five hundredth year there.

The longest time on record that anyone had been trapped in the World of Time was one thousand years. No one had come close to a five-digit year count, let alone ten. That was what scared her. The thought that Allen could survive in that hell for a billion years and be so casual about it was frightening.

"Hmm… Even considering the extraordinary strength of the Spirit Core residing within him, there's something strange about Allen." She had finally come to recognize the unusualness of Allen's nature.

"Well, I certainly didn't see that coming. I need to contact Dalia right away..."

Reia got to work contacting Allen's mother, Dalia Rodol.

■

It was the day after I heard the revelation about the 100-Million-Year Button from Chairwoman Reia. Afternoon classes were over, and Class 1-A had returned to the classroom for afternoon homeroom.

"Hello, boys and girls, nice job getting through another hard day of classes! I can see you all are starting to get fatigued, but you're young and spry! You can overcome it!" Chairwoman Reia proclaimed, whacking the blackboard and telling us to grit our way through like she always did. That was her way of encouraging us.

Everyone's been tired lately... Our classes were the same as ever, but I could see the exhaustion on my classmates' faces.

Lia and Rose were no exception. I asked the two of them about it indirectly to find out why they were so tired, and they said that Soul Attire class had become especially difficult. All they had done in class until now was talk and negotiate with their Spirit Core to get it to share its power, but lately their requests for more power had caused their Spirit Cores to show violent resistance. They were now having to clash with their Spirit Core every class as a result, and it was taking a great mental toll on them.

I suppose I've been lucky in that regard. He had never once shared even a drop of his power with me, not from the very beginning. *The day I show weakness by trying to talk or negotiate with him, he'll just punch me as hard as he can and send me back to the real world.* I had been fighting my Spirit Core from day one, so while everyone else was at the end of their rope, I alone felt full of energy. I was already used to mental fatigue.

Everyone is working so hard... I need to follow their example and push myself harder than ever before! My motivation for training had been growing significantly as of late. I was also lasting much longer while fighting *him* in the Soul World. Now that I had obtained the darkness, I was able to reliably block his attacks. That was enormous progress.

This pitch-black darkness is a really useful power. I could use it simultaneously as protection and as a weapon. Coating my body with it gave me strong armor, concentrating it into my sword created a fearsomely sharp mock black sword, and focusing it onto my wounds healed me instantly in most scenarios.

But what kind of power does my Soul Attire have? I was still a long way from learning what my Soul Attire was capable of. The thought alone got my heart racing and caused a smile to form on my face. *Ha-ha, I can't wait for classes tomorrow!* I thought.

"Attention, everyone! Normally I would dismiss you right now, but I have an important matter to discuss today!" Chairwoman Reia said, clearing her throat. "It's that time of year again…it's time for the Thousand Blade Festival! I'm sure plenty of you have heard about it from your upperclassmen in clubs, but I'll give you a simple explanation just in case!"

She began her explanation about the Thousand Blade Festival.

"The Thousand Blade Festival is a festival held once a year at our school. It's very popular, as you might expect from one of the Elite Five Academies! Lots of people come from the general public every year to participate, among them young practitioners of the blade who may apply here in the future. You all should be proud of your position as Thousand Blade students and do your best to have fun!"

I had heard most of that from Shii, Lilim, and Tirith.

"The Thousand Blade Festival is in just two weeks. I want you all to decide on your event right now. Please raise your hand if you have a good idea! I'll allow you to put on any event you like, so don't hold back!"

We spent some time sharing ideas before eventually narrowing it down to five candidates: a cosplay café, a class movie, a minigame tournament, a homemade ramzac restaurant, and an outdoor practice-swing meet. They all sounded like a lot of fun, and choosing just one was going to be difficult. The outdoor practice-swing meet was my personal favorite.

"Hmm, not sure how this one made the ballot… Eh, whatever." Chairwoman Reia handed out voting paper to the entire class and set a ballot box on her desk. "Place your paper into this box once you've decided what to vote for!"

We submitted our votes one by one.

"All right, that's everyone. Let's go ahead and count the ballots!" the chairwoman declared, opening the box and tallying the votes without a moment's delay.

The result was as followed:

Cosplay café—sixteen votes.

Class movie—six votes.

Minigame tournament—four votes.

Homemade ramzac restaurant—three votes.

Outdoor practice-swing meet—one vote.

The cosplay café received the most votes, so it was chosen for Class 1-A's event.

"How the heck?!"

We had decided by majority rule, so I had no complaints with the result. There was one thing that hurt me, though—the outdoor practice-swing meet I proposed only received one vote. I was obviously the one who voted for it, which meant it essentially got zero votes.

How do they not see how much fun performing practice swings with swordsmen from outside the academy would be?! It seemed I had done a poor job of explaining the appeal of the outdoor practice-swing meet to everyone.

I'll try again next year. This wouldn't be my last Thousand Blade Festival. I was going to try again next year with an upgraded outdoor practice-swing meet.

The chairwoman spoke up as the desire for revenge burned inside me.

"Okay class, go ahead and start your preparations!"

""""Yes, ma'am!""""

At the chairwoman's direction, we started preparing our cosplay café.

■

Class 1-A spent the next two weeks using our after-school hours to prepare for the Thousand Blade Festival. Deciding on costumes was the first task. The girls were getting very excited looking at a catalogue.

"Hey, I think this would look *so* good on you, Lia!"

"I-I don't know. That skirt looks a little short…"

"Oh, don't worry about that! You can just put on leggings!"

"Th-that doesn't make it much better!"

The guys had absolutely no sway in this conversation.

"What about you, Rose? Do you see anything you'd like to wear?"

"Hmm… I'm thinking about this one."

"Huh?! That's surprisingly daring…"

"Really? Looks normal enough to me."

Rose nonchalantly picked the outfit she liked.

I-I wonder if that's gonna be okay… Given how much skin she exposed with her personal clothes, I was a little worried about what kind of outfit she would pick.

While the girls were having fun picking costumes, the guys were hard at work mass-producing colorful origami rings for decoration. At first, we were all excitedly discussing which girls we couldn't wait to see in costume, but…

Cut, fold, glue. Cut, fold, glue. Cut, fold, glue.

The talk gradually died down as we performed the same rote actions over and over and over again, and after about three hours we were reduced to nothing more than miserable origami-ring-making machines.

"Hey, Allen. Can you come over here for a second?"

The monotony was broken when a smiling group of girls called me over.

"What is it?"

"We were brainstorming what you should wear!"

"I-I'm going to dress up, too?!"

"Of course, silly! We have to give you a cool outfit to rope in the female customers!"

They began to cheerfully present to me a variety of outfits. *I really don't think there will be any demand for that.* They were clearly eager to pick something out for me, though; I didn't want to put a damper on their fun by protesting.

We moved on to the menu once the costumes were chosen. This was going to be a café, so we needed drinks and some light meals.

"We should have coffee, café latte, café au lait, and cappuccino. I think macchiato would be nice, too!"

"Hey, don't forget about carbonated drinks!"

"Oh, right! What about the food?"

"I want toast, spaghetti with meat sauce, omelette over rice, and hashed beef rice, at least."

"Sounds good to me! Let's do pancakes and coffee jelly for dessert!"

"Hey, this is shaping up to be a proper café!"

The boys and girls of the class excitedly shared their ideas.

"Excuse me?! Wanna say that again?!"

"Like I said, nobody wants that kind of menu at a café!"

Meanwhile, Tessa was arguing with a female student. *What's going on?* I decided to listen in on their conversation.

"We need to add white rice, *hijiki* seaweed, dried sardines, boiled seasonal greens, and pickled daikon radish! What's a café without the vegetarian cuisine of the Slice Iron Style?!"

"That's absurd! This is a cosplay café!"

"Oh come on, you just don't get it! Hey, Allen! What do you think?"

Tessa suddenly roped me into the argument.

"W-well... I think you're wrong on this one, Tessa," I answered honestly.

That kind of vegetarian cuisine didn't exactly fit a cosplay café.

"Grrr... Fine. I won't argue with you, Allen. I guess I have to back down." He grimaced, reluctantly giving up.

Once we had the costumes and the menu worked out, all that was left was cooking practice.

"Ugh, I hate omelette over rice. It's so difficult to make..."

"Shoot! Why can't I make the eggs nice and round?! There's something wrong with this frying pan!"

"Ah-ha-ha... I don't normally cook, so this is a little embarrassing."

The girls in the class were doing their best to make fluffy eggs, but it wasn't going well. Rose was struggling most of all. It didn't seem like any of them really knew how to cook.

I should be able to help out a little with this, I thought, deciding to give them some advice for making omelette over rice.

"I actually have a trick for flipping eggs cleanly. All you have to do is insert the eggs, stir them thoroughly over the frying pan, and then when it comes time to flip them, be conscious about tearing them away from the pan. That makes it easy."

The girls followed my advice.

"Oh my god! ...I'm impressed, Allen. I can't believe you're well-versed in the culinary arts, too!"

"Whoa, I didn't know you could do it that way! You're the best, Allen!"

"Wow, it really worked! Thanks, Allen. I'm amazed that you can cook, too."

The girls looked at me with envy as they each succeeded at making perfectly fluffy omelettes.

"You're welcome. Honestly, I went through a bit of a cooking phase," I responded.

The citizens of Goza Village were totally self-sufficient. Everyone needed to be able to do fundamental things like harvesting vegetables, taking care of livestock, and cooking on their own in order to eat. Even more importantly, I spent about a million years in the World of Time devoting myself to making food. I was a better cook than most boys as a result.

The two weeks leading up to the Thousand Blade Festival were busy yet fun, and they passed by in a flash.

■

It was the day of the Thousand Blade Festival. Class 1-A gathered in the classroom at half-past eight—thirty minutes before the start of the festival—and got to work preparing the café for opening. As Tessa and a group of students were getting the kitchen ready for cooking, I was in the men's locker room changing into my costume.

"Let's see, this goes here..."

I dressed myself according to some instructions that had been scribbled on a note. My outfit consisted of a blue *haori* jacket with a white wave design, an elegant gray *hakama* skirt, and simple black sandals.

"I think this is called a samurai costume?"

Samurai were a minority population found in a certain country to the Far East who were known for their unique style of swordcraft. They were normally gentle and preferred to avoid conflict, but their smiling faces belied their immense skill with the blade.

"There we go."

I finished putting on the samurai outfit and studied my reflection closely in the mirror.

"...Yep, I'm really gonna stand out in this."

I felt a sudden pang of nerves now that the festival was about to start. I knew, however, that I couldn't possibly pull out after all the hard work we had put in.

"Haah..." I let out a long breath to calm myself.

...Oh yeah. I need to remember this is a festival; dressing up like this is nothing unusual. I was probably going to stand out in this outfit, but no one was going to find that weird. At least, I hoped that would be the case.

"All I need to do is act confidently, and I'll be fine!"

Ready to face the world in my samurai outfit, I headed for the 1-A classroom where everyone was waiting. I passed through a hallway full of students preparing for the festival, and opened the classroom door.

"H-hey, Allen! Wow, I knew it would look great on you!"

"You look really handsome! You're going to be soooo popular!"

The female students all complimented my outfit. I didn't have much experience being praised by girls, so I was unsure of what to say in response.

"Huh...? O-oh, uh... Thanks."

Just after my uncertain reply, the classroom door opened behind me and Lia walked in wearing her costume.

"W-wow!"

"Hot damn... Is that level of cuteness allowed?!"

"Oh my god... My heart can't take it..."

The guys reacted dramatically to Lia's appearance, but she walked straight toward me without so much as a glance at any of them.

"H-how do I look, Allen?" she asked, her cheeks reddening as she showed me her cute costume.

She was wearing a black dress with a white, frilly apron—it was a maid costume. The outfit complemented her beautiful blond hair and facial features. To say she was adorable was an understatement.

"I-I think you look really cute...," I stammered.

"R-really... Thanks!" she responded, smiling shyly.

Lia couldn't possibly look any more adorable in this maid outfit. One thing about it worried me, though. I looked hesitantly toward her legs. *Is she okay with that?*

Her skirt was shockingly short. It was tiny enough that a little wind could lift it up and reveal everything underneath. *It's probably not the best idea for a guy to point this out, but...* I felt like I had no choice but to say something.

"U-uh, Lia... Is *that* okay?" I asked, pointing at her skirt discreetly to avoid mentioning it out loud.

"Mm-hmm, it's not a problem. Look!" she said, lifting both sides of her skirt.

"Wh-whoa, Lia?!" I panicked and covered my eyes with both hands. An accidental crack between my fingers, however, gave me a view of the inside of her skirt... But strangely, there was nothing to see.

"Huh?"

Upon closer inspection, her upper legs were still totally covered. She was actually wearing short-shorts made to look like a miniskirt.

"...You're a perv, Allen."

"H-huh? N-no, I didn't mean to look, i-it just happened...," I stuttered under Lia's glare. She then laughed mischievously.

"Hmm-hmm, I'm just kidding. Did I surprise you? This is apparently called a culotte skirt. The girls in the class assured me that it would be okay," she shared, and spun around on the spot. Her skirt fluttered up into the air, but because it was closed on the inside, nothing was revealed underneath.

"Wow, that's good…," I said, feeling relieved. I didn't like the thought of anyone looking at Lia with indecent gazes.

"…Does that make you feel better?" she asked, bending down and peering into my face.

"Yeah, much better," I responded.

"Hee-hee, thanks."

"…? Why are you thanking me?"

"That just made me feel kind of happy."

Our conversation was interrupted when the door behind us flew open noisily.

"Good morning, Allen."

"Hey, Rose. Good morning… Huh?!"

Rose was wearing a bunny-ear headband, a white cotton tail, a black leotard that bared her shoulders and upper chest, and fishnet tights over her legs. She was dressed as a bunny girl, and she pulled off the getup spectacularly.

"How do I look? Amazing, right?" she asked bombastically.

"Y-yeah, you look great, but…are you really okay wearing that?" I responded timidly.

"What do you mean?"

"U-um, well…you're showing a lot of your shoulders, and your, um, ch-chest area…"

"Oh, this is nothing. It's not too different from what I normally wear."

"…You've got a point."

Her personal wear consisted of a top that exposed her lower chest all the way down to her stomach and short shorts that liberally exposed her legs. What she was wearing now really wasn't that different. I supposed it wasn't an issue.

"That's a samurai costume, right, Allen?" asked Lia.

"Oh, that makes sense," said Rose.

They both inspected my costume from head to toe.

"It's really cool. It looks great on you!" Lia beamed.

"Yeah, it's tasteful. The calming blue suits you very well," Rose commented.

They both nodded satisfactorily.

"Ah-ha-ha, thank you."

We continued to talk, and before we knew it, there were only three minutes left before the start of the festival. Our preparation was already complete—the portable microwave, cooking utensils, foodstuffs, tableware, and decorations were already in place.

"I-I'm a little nervous...," admitted Lia.

"Being a little on edge isn't a bad thing," assured Rose.

"Ah-ha-ha, that's true," I said.

Lia, Rose, and I would be the waiters, and our job was to memorize the menu and learn simple serving etiquette. We'd finished all our preparation last night, so all we could do now was wait for the start of the festival.

Thirty seconds before opening, Chairwoman Reia's voice sounded over the academy's intercom.

"Good morning, boys and girls! This is Chairwoman Reia Lasnote. You've done a great job preparing your events in two short weeks. Now all you have to do is demonstrate the results of your hard work! I now declare the start of the Thousand Blade Festival!"

I heard loud cheers outside the classroom in response to the chairwoman's announcement.

H-huh? I looked outside the window and saw an enormous crowd of people closing in on the school buildings.

"Th-that's so many people...," Lia remarked.

"I guess that's to be expected for one of the Elite Five Academies," Rose added.

Just as Lia and Rose had said, there were a ton of people outside; it was enough to remind me of Holy Street in Drestia, the Merchant Town.

A moment later, the first customers arrived at the Class 1-A cosplay café.

"Excuse me, we have a party of three. Are you open yet?"

It was a group of three girls.

"Yes, ma'am. We ask all customers at this café to choose a waiter dressed in cosplay. Which one would you prefer?" Tessa said with a natural smile perfect for greeting customers. He was in charge of reception, and he delivered his lines without falter.

Good job, Tessa! His confidence showed how hard he had worked when no one was looking.

"Hmm... We would like 'Allen,' please."

The three girls pointed at a portrait of my face that had been placed at reception. I greeted them with a smile every bit as natural as Tessa's.

"Welcome. Thank you for choosing our café as your first stop this morning. Please, follow me," I said, and escorted them to their seats. "What would you like to order?" I asked in a calm tone so as not to rush them.

"Hmm... Can I please have honey toast and a café latte?"

"Let's see... I'd like an egg sandwich and coffee."

"Um... I'm really hungry, so I guess I'll go with omelette over rice and a latte."

"Thank you. I have honey toast and a latte, an egg sandwich and coffee, and omelette over rice and a café latte. Is that correct?"

I took quick notes as I listened and completed the orders by reading their choices back to them. The students in charge of cooking would now make the food, and I would finish this job by carrying it to the customers.

All right, that went perfectly! This job was going to be easy.

I didn't think that for long.

"Allen, another four customers just chose you!"

"Understood!"

"Lia, please show this customer to a table!"

"Okay!"

"Five more people for you, Allen!"

"All right, please wait a moment...!"

"Rose, two for you."

"Okay, got it."

"Allen, we have a group of seven for you!"

"O-okay...!"

For some reason I didn't understand, a disproportionate amount of people were picking me. They were all groups of female customers, and they always tried to make conversation with me after I escorted them to their tables. Taking their orders was a difficult task.

This must be the result of some kind of special girls' network... Female customers called more female customers until our cosplay café took on the appearance of a women-only restaurant.

I spent the next three hours or so serving the endless flood of female customers, until finally our shifts came to an end. Lia, Rose, and I were in charge of serving during the morning shift, and we were free for the rest of the day.

After changing into our uniforms in the locker room, we decided to walk around and look at the other classes' events. We already knew what our first destination was going to be—Class 2-A's haunted house.

"H-hey, Allen? Are you sure you want to do this?" Lia asked hesitantly.

"N-now is the time if you want to turn back...," Rose stuttered.

"Ah-ha-ha, but we already told the president, Lilim, and Tirith that we're coming," I answered.

Despite her kind features, Shii was the type to hold a grudge. If we stood her up, we'd regret it later. *Also, I'm simply excited for it.* According to the president, it was so good last year that over ten people had fainted. I was actually looking forward to seeing their setup.

We pushed our way through the crowd until we reached Class 2-A's room. It was a sight to behold.

"Wow, this is really impressive," I commented.

Their huge, haunted mansion made full use of classrooms 2-A through 2-C. You couldn't tell that the space had ever been occupied by classrooms. The exterior was painted black and covered by unsettling, serpentine ivy, and there were scratch marks and dark-red bloodstains strewn throughout.

They did a great job on the atmosphere. I thought it was safe to get my hopes up.

I glanced over at my companions.

""...""

Lia and Rose were holding hands, both pale-faced and stiff. We hadn't even gone inside yet, and the exterior already had them overwhelmed.

"Hey, if you're scared you can just say—" I began.

""I'm not scared!""

As stubborn as ever, the two girls both interrupted me to insist they were okay. Their trembling legs couldn't have made it any more obvious that they were bluffing.

"Okay, okay. I'm sorry for even suggesting it."

I knew full well how obstinate they could be about owning up to their weaknesses. I gave up on trying to convince them and approached reception.

"Excuse me, we're a group of three students."

"Thank you very much. You may enter. Please watch your step inside."

I paid the entrance fee and led the frightened girls into the haunted mansion that Shii, Lilim, and Tirith were so proud of.

"This is reception. The target has entered the venue. President, I leave the rest to you."

"This is Shii. Roger that... Hmm-hmm, he's finally here. It's time for me to exact my revenge, Allen!"

The door opened into a small, dim room.

"What's this...?"

There was a large poster pinned to an old bulletin board on the wall in front of us. I could see in the faint light that it contained warnings for the haunted house.

PLEASE REFRAIN FROM RUNNING INSIDE THE BUILDING.

PLEASE STAY WHERE YOU ARE IF YOU FEEL UNWELL. A SERVANT WILL COME TO GET YOU.

PLEASE BEAR IN MIND THAT REMOTE CONTROL SOUL ATTIRE WILL BE USED FOR CERTAIN DISPLAYS.

PROCEED WITH CAUTION.

The warnings were written like this was a real haunted house, and reading made me even more excited.

"Lia, Rose."

"Y-yes?!"

"Wh-what is it?!"

Just saying their names caused them to practically leap out of their shoes. *Are they really going to be okay?* I was more than a little worried. They had both stubbornly insisted that they weren't afraid, though, so there was nothing I could do about it.

"We've read the notice, so do you want to go ahead and start?" I asked, pointing toward the only door in the room.

"Y-yeah, sure..."

"R-right..."

They both nodded gravely with meek expressions. Seeing that, I opened the door. It led to a narrow corridor with black curtains on either side. Pale blue lights placed throughout lit the pathway and showed us the suggested route.

"Wh-whoa... Th-th-this looks kind of ominous. Not that I'm frightened or anything!" Lia insisted.

"Sh-Shii, Lilim, and Tirith did a really good job... I'm not scared either, though!" Rose claimed.

"Ah-ha-ha, yeah they really nailed the atmosphere," I responded, finding their bluffing amusing. I took one step forward into the hallway, and heard the door behind us lock with a click.

""EEEEK!!!""

Lia and Rose both screamed incoherently.

"Hmm... Looks like they locked the entrance," I observed.

I tried multiple times to open the door we'd just passed through, but it didn't budge.

"Wh-wh-what should we do, Allen?!" Lia cried.

"W-we're trapped in here!!" Rose shouted.

They both shook violently in panic. It was rare to see them shaken like this; it was kind of cute.

"It's okay. Let's just calm down," I reassured them.

"Whoo... Haa... O-okay. Thanks."

"Phew... Sorry, that surprised me a bit."

I waited as they both regained their composure.

"Wanna get moving?" I asked, and we finally started to make our way through the haunted house.

I walked in front with Lia and Rose behind me to either side. They were both clinging to the sleeves of my uniform, which made walking very difficult. I couldn't exactly tell them to let go of me, though, given how they were both trembling with fright.

That locking sound was a really effective way to set people on edge. Humans naturally felt anxiety and fear when locked up. In light of that, locking the door was a simple yet effective way to kick off the haunted house.

I'm pretty sure Tirith was the director. A quick scan of our surroundings revealed a cracked mirror, a single slipper, a half-open locker, and many other small props placed about the area to indirectly stir fear in the hearts of visitors. *It's all so well-thought-out for creating a spooky environment.* I could see how this haunted house caused over ten people to faint last year.

Ha-ha, I'm getting pretty excited!

We walked down the narrow, dark passageway until a student dressed as an old man with a crooked back slowly walked toward us with a cane.

"Hey, you three! Are you still alive?!" he said, continuing without waiting for a response. "We deceased souls are tied to a keystone deep within this mansion, and cannot move on to the afterlife... I have a request for you. Would you be so kind as to find the Disenchantment Talisman located somewhere in this mansion and affix it to the keystone?"

It sounded like we would have to grant his wish and help the ghosts trapped in this mansion move on to the afterlife to complete the haunted house.

"Some souls like me have maintained their sanity, but others have turned evil and will attack you on sight. Please be careful," he warned, walking off somewhere.

"D-Disenchantment Talisman?" Lia repeated.

"I see, we need to find that first," Rose said.

My friends were getting sucked into the haunted house's storyline now that we had been given a clear objective.

"All right, want to start looking for the talisman?" I asked.

"Yeah."

"Sure."

Now that they had gotten more used to the atmosphere of this place, the girls moved up to walk by my side. We made our way left and right through the narrow corridors and emerged into a spacious room.

There's definitely going to be a gimmick to scare us in here. I started to warily make my way across the chamber. Just then, the room was filled with the tremendous sound of wings flapping and crows cawing.

""Eek?!""

Lia and Rose both shrieked and clung to me, but the show wasn't over yet. Cold wind blew violently from all directions, and bloody dolls attached to the ceiling began to rattle.

""Aaaah, aaaaah...""

Is the next one gonna come from below? While their eyes were fixed above, I calmly looked down. *The dolls are clearly supposed to attract our attention. That's a typical way to guide someone's eyes in a certain direction.*

My estimation was right on the money. I strained my eyes and saw bloody hands crawling toward us unsteadily to grab our legs. This must have been one of the displays utilizing remote-control Soul Attire that we'd been warned about.

I knew they would try to get us from below. These hands look really realistic... Were they made with clay or something? I thought, easily dodging the creeping extremities. Less than a second later, they grabbed Lia's and Rose's legs while they were distracted by the dolls on the ceiling.

""AAAAAAAAAAH?!""

Caught completely unawares, they both unleashed ear-piercing screams.

"C-calm down, guys! It's okay! They're just fake hands!" I informed them, giving away the trick.

"O-oh, th-th-they are...," Lia stuttered.

"Th-that surprised me...," Rose admitted.

Their voices quivered, and there were tears in the corners of their eyes; that must have really frightened them.

"Hey, take a moment to steady yourselves. Slow, deep breaths," I advised.

"O-okay..."

"R-right... Good idea..."

They had truly panicked.

""Hee-hee-hoo... Hee-hee-hoo...""

That wasn't quite the breathing technique I've had in mind... *Well, anything's fine as long as it calms them down.*

Then, just as they had started to regain their composure, a scroll fell from the ceiling.

""Eeek?!""

I picked it up and unrolled it to look inside.

"Oh, it's a map."

A rough sketch of the haunted house had been drawn on the map. There was a red X on it, likely indicating the location of the Disenchantment Talisman.

The scares came from above, below, and then above again. This room was skillfully designed to direct your attention to catch you off guard.

"All right, let's get moving," I said.

""O-okay...""

Neither one of them would be able to fall asleep tonight if we lingered here. *It might already be too late for that.*

We resumed our search for the Disenchantment Talisman.

"Geez, Allen's good. He saw through that trick entirely..."

"What should we do, Shii?! He might be even tougher than we feared!"

"I don't know if anything will frighten him at this rate...!"

"N-no need to panic yet. We still have plenty of scares left!"

■

As we continued to make our way through the haunted house, the girls grew more distressed with every step. Lia was clinging tightly to my right arm and Rose to my left, and they weren't showing any signs of letting go. That made walking a challenge, but that was nowhere close to being the most stressful thing about it.

......

I couldn't help being hyper-aware of the soft sensation pressing against my arms. I had tried to separate myself multiple times, but they weren't having it. Feeling incredibly uncomfortable, I continued through the narrow corridors with them by my side until we emerged into a wide-open space.

This has to be where we're supposed to go. This was the spot indicated by the red X on the map.

Man, this is really well made. The detail is amazing. The room was made to look like a temple. The main hall of the temple was positioned in the center, and there were giant statues to either side of it. An offering box decorated with white slips of paper had been placed in front of the hall. Those were most likely the Disenchantment Talismans.

"L-look, Allen! We found it!" Lia shouted.

"Yes! Now we can get out of here!" Rose cheered.

The two girls both rushed forward happily after finally finding what we were looking for… But this couldn't have been a more obvious place for a scare.

"H-hey, wait!" I called out immediately, but they were too distracted at the prospect of completing the haunted house to hear me.

"We did it! We got the Disenchantment Talisman!"

"All right, now all we need to do is find the keystone!"

They both smiled with satisfaction after grabbing a talisman.

"*Give it baaaaaaaaaaaaack!*"

Suddenly, a girl covered in blood jumped out of the offering box.

""Aaa…AAAAAAAAAAHHHHHHHHHHHH!!!""

Overwhelmed by fear, they took off sprinting deeper into the haunted house.

"L-Lia?! Rose?!"

…They were gone. It was unlikely they were in any danger; this was just an attraction made by our upperclassmen.

"They both tried so hard…" I was impressed that they had managed to keep it together for so long considering how easily they were scared by this kind of thing. Admiring their determination, I continued through the haunted house alone and enjoyed the various tricks my upperclassmen had prepared.

"Is this the end?"

I slapped the Disenchantment Talisman onto the keystone deep within the mansion. Tranquil music you might hear at a church began to play, and a door behind the keystone opened slowly. It looked like the exit.

That was even more fun than I expected. I headed for the light of the entrance. I had completed the haunted house.

"BOOO!"

The president jumped out from behind a pillar dressed in white like a ghost.

"Hey, President. You all did such a good job. I loved all the elaborate props and how the traps were designed to catch people by surprise. It was so much fun," I said, sharing my honest feelings.

"Th-thanks... Wait, don't give me that!" She looked caught off guard for a moment, but then her expression quickly turned petulant. "How were you not scared by a single one of our tricks?! Even what I did just now shouldn't have gotten *no* reaction out of you!" she vented in a fit of rage.

"Ah-ha-ha, sorry...," I responded, smiling awkwardly and shifting my feet.

The jump scare at the end had been basic but effective. They lulled their guests into a false sense of security by making them think the haunted house was over, only to attack when they least expected it. I had been ready for it, though.

"I caught a whiff of your nice scent in the air, so I figured you were hiding behind the pillar," I explained.

It was human nature for the unexpected to surprise you. Conversely, you weren't likely to be caught off guard by something you saw coming.

"M-my 'nice scent'...?" The president blushed. She must have been embarrassed to have made a mistake.

"Anyway, I need to find Lia and Rose. See you later."

I'd managed to get through Class 2-A's mega-sized three-classroom haunted house without issue.

∎

After ending my pleasant jaunt through the haunted house, I stretched out some of the kinks in my back and neck.

"Nrgh…"

The light from the windows felt bright after being in that dimly lit spook-fest for so long.

"All right, I need to find Lia and Rose."

I started by thinking of places they were likely to be. *That would be the cafeteria for Lia, and the training ground for Rose.* I ran through the most probable spots in my head, and was about to go to the cafeteria when Lia and Rose emerged from the girls' bathroom in front of me. They had stayed together instead of running off in random directions.

"Lia, Rose! Thank goodness!" I said, waving and rushing toward them.

""…I wasn't crying.""

They both mumbled something I couldn't hear.

"…Huh? Sorry, I didn't hear you. Can you repeat that?"

""I said I wasn't crying!""

"O-oh… Don't worry, I believe you."

I realized as soon as I saw them that they had both been crying in the bathroom. Their red, puffy eyes made it obvious.

"…Okay."

"…Good."

They both spun away from me and fell silent.

"   "
…

"   "
…

"   "
…

An awkward quiet stretched between us. *I need to think of something to cheer them up.* It was the day of the Thousand Blade Festival and experiencing it while depressed would be a waste. *What would be a good way to help get their minds off the haunted house…? Yeah, I guess that's the best option.*

"Oh yeah, I heard that Class 2-F is running a chocolate banana stand," I said.

"…!"

Lia's eyebrows twitched. *Did that entice her?* She was a gourmand. Playing the food card was always a surefire way to cheer her up when she was feeling down.

"I'm feeling a little hungry, so do you want to go get some?" I asked, giving one final push.

"...Sure." Lia nodded.

"Awesome, it's a plan. What about you, Rose? I think getting some food will be a nice break."

"Yeah, you're right... I'll have one, too," she answered, agreeing with my plan as well.

Having reached a decision, we began to walk toward Class 2-F.

■

We took the long way through the halls to avoid passing by the haunted house and arrived at our destination.

"Wow, it's really busy," I observed.

A line of more than ten people stretched in front of the classroom. By standing on my tiptoes, I was just able to see where the chocolate bananas were being made. The students were applying warm, melted chocolate to the bananas, and then adding red, yellow, green, white, and black chocolate sprinkles as the finishing touch.

"Those look so good!" Lia exclaimed, her eyes lighting up like a child's.

"Let's get in line," I said.

"Okay!"

We took our place at the end of the line, and our turn arrived sooner than expected.

"Thank you for waiting. Welcome to our chocolate banana stand, Thousand Banana!"

The female student taking orders greeted us kindly.

"Um, can I please have one chocolate banana?" I asked.

"I'll have one, too," Rose said.

"Hmm... I don't know if we're gonna stop anywhere else later, so I guess I'll start with five, please," requested Lia, holding up five fingers and giving an order fit for a king.

"D-did you say five? Not one?"

The girl was taken off guard by Lia's ridiculous order. She'd probably assumed she misheard Lia, or that Lia had misspoken. I couldn't blame her for that; no one would think a girl as slim as Lia would ask for that many.

"...? Yes, five please," Lia repeated, looking puzzled. She had no self-awareness about her enormous appetite and didn't realize there was something unusual about ordering five chocolate bananas for one person.

"C-coming right up..."

After confirming that there had been no mistake, the girl rushed into the kitchen to convey our orders.

She's ordering five just to get herself started in case we eat more later... Lia never changed. Even feeling down about the haunted house had done nothing to weaken her appetite.

Once we received our seven chocolate bananas, we moved to a spot away from all the crowds. We all took our first bites of chocolate-covered fruit goodness together.

"Wow, this is tasty," I commented.

"Mmm! Chocolate and bananas are so good together, it should be illegal!" Lia gushed.

"Sweet foods sure are comforting," Rose said.

Lia and Rose looked blissful as they indulged in their chocolate bananas. I breathed a sigh of relief as I glanced at them in the corners of my eyes. *Looks like they're okay.* The chocolate bananas had driven the trauma of the haunted house from their minds.

I'll have to stop them next year. Shii, Lilim, and Tirith were second years, which meant they had one more Thousand Blade Festival left. I was certain they would come back next year with an even scarier haunted house. If Lia and Rose once again insisted they weren't frightened and tried to go through it again, I was going to counter with this year's experience to shut them down.

Life really is unpredictable. Just a few months ago, I had been in hell. I was loathed, ridiculed, and straight-up ignored. I'd had no friends, and no one gave me the time of day. My world had been limited to the small, isolated Grand Swordcraft Academy.

One time, I'd returned to Goza Village intending to tell Mom about how I was being bullied. *But I couldn't bring myself to say it.* Her hands were covered in mud and her forehead was glistening with sweat—she was working so hard to pay my tuition, and I didn't want to increase her burden. I'd just returned to my dorm and resumed my miserable school life.

Look at me now. The Reject Swordsman was now attending Thousand Blade Academy, one of the famous Elite Five Academies. I had made invaluable friends in Lia and Rose, and not just them—I also had Tessa and the rest of Class 1-A, my friends in the Student Council, and many kind upperclassmen. I'd found myself surrounded by friends in no time flat.

Man, I'm having the time of my life... If only these days could last forever—I had found myself thinking that a lot lately, as if I were an old man who didn't have long left to live.

"...Is something wrong, Allen?" Lia asked, staring at me with a concerned expression.

"Huh? Oh, sorry... I just zoned out a bit," I answered.

"Did something bad happen? You looked really sad."

"I did?"

That's strange. I was just thinking about how happy I was right now... I didn't know why I would've looked sad.

"Do you want another?" Lia asked, offering me one of her chocolate bananas.

It's not every day you see Lia offer to share some of her own food. I must have looked like I was in real pain.

"Thanks. I appreciate the thought, but I'm good. Anyway, it would be a waste to spend the whole festival sitting around. Let's go look at the other events!" I said, standing up energetically and trying to lift the slightly heavy mood.

"Yeah, you're right!"

"Sounds good."

We then enjoyed a variety of events including target practice, ring toss, a lottery, a stamp rally, and more. Lia, meanwhile, ate everything she laid her eyes on—candy apples, grilled corn on the cob, hot dogs, *yakisoba*, crêpes, you name it. I continue to be amazed at her ability to pack in so much yet maintain her figure

"Ah-ha-ha, this is so much fun Allen!"

"There's nothing like a good festival."

Lia and Rose genuinely enjoyed the day, smiling all the while as we checked out the events.

"What's that?" Lia asked, looking at a crowd that had formed in the middle of the schoolyard.

"Good question…," I responded.

There was an elevated stage set up in the middle of the crowd, on top of which two swordsmen were staring each other down.

"Hmm, that must be Class 3-B's Dojo Challenge event," Rose said, looking at her pamphlet.

""Dojo challenge?""

"Yeah. It says if you can defeat a third year named Jean Bael and his spectacular swordcraft, you win a luxurious prize. Basically, it's a chance to try and best a swordsman from another school," Rose explained.

"Oh, okay."

"Interesting."

Spectacular swordcraft, huh…? That caught my interest as a swordsman.

"Hmm, that sounds pretty fun. Let's check it out," Lia suggested.

"I'm kind of curious to see how good he is," Rose said.

They both had a competitive glint in their eyes. The "spectacular swordcraft" claim must have gotten their attention as well.

"How about we go there next, then?" I asked.

"Let's do it!" Lia responded.

"Sure," added Rose.

We passed through Thousand Blade's main school building and arrived at the stage in the middle of the schoolyard.

"That's enough! Jean Bael is the winner!"

It sounded like a duel just ended.

"Amazing… He's forty-nine for forty-nine now…"

"I can see why he's the president of the Swordcraft Club. He's really good…"

"Crap, they never intended for anyone to win a prize, did they…?"

I heard a few people complaining amid the cheering crowd. Those people had injuries of varying sizes; they must have challenged Jean Bael and lost.

Forty-nine out of forty-nine… He was undefeated, and that was while performing all of these matches consecutively without rest. *Looks like his "spectacular swordcraft" claim is justified.*

"L-look at that, Allen!"

Lia suddenly tapped my shoulder and pointed at a clear box with the label LUXURIOUS PRIZES. There were a number of goods inside including gift certificates and a sharp-looking sword.

I'm pretty sure Rose just said that if you succeed at the Dojo Challenge you get to pick from among those goods, I thought, staring absent-mindedly at the prizes. "Oh, I see." I quickly realized what had Lia so excited.

"I-it's a hippo! It's a stuffed hippo, Allen!" she exclaimed, tugging excitedly at my sleeve.

"Ah-ha-ha, that it is."

Lia had a real fondness for cute things. She especially loved stuffed animals, and our room was packed with them. I occasionally saw her talking to her favorite stuffed bear. I always pretended I hadn't seen anything, for her sake and my own.

"Hey, Allen… Can you win me that doll?" she requested, looking down bashfully.

"Why can't you win it yourself, Lia?" Rose asked. That was a very good question.

"I-I just want Allen to… You know… I just think it would be really nice as a present!" Lia yelled, blushing furiously.

"Ah-ha-ha, got it. I don't know if I'll be able to, but I'll do my best to win it for you," I said.

"…! Th-thanks!"

I pushed my way through the crowd to sign up for the Dojo Challenge.

"Excuse me, can I please try the Dojo Challenge?" I asked the male student at reception.

"Sure thing. We'll just get you signed up... Whuh?! Y-you're finally here!" he shouted, leaping back in surprise.

"...Huh?" I said, confused.

"Jean! It's Allen Rodol! He came to destroy you, just like we thought he would!" the receptionist yelled loudly, and the entire crowd turned toward me.

"Ha, so you came after all. Guess the stories are true—you'll do anything for money," the swordsman on the stage, Jean Bael, said while glaring at me.

D-did he say I'd do "anything for money"? It seemed like another terrible rumor had been fabricated about me. The tales about me were always embellished, and some of them were truly shocking to hear. *I tried to correct people at first.* The gossip had gotten completely out of hand recently, however, so I had abandoned the effort entirely.

"Take the stage, Allen. I've been wanting to cross blades with you," he declared, pointing his bamboo sword at me. I accepted his challenge and climbed onto the stage, and a moment later a female announcer spoke up for everyone to hear.

"All right, the person we've all been waiting for has finally graced the stage! You all know him—it's Allen Rodooooool! He's a rare talent who recently defeated the Wonder Child, Idora Luksmaria of White Lily Girls Academy! Many call him the greatest first year in the country, and he attends this very academy!"

She moved on to Jean's introduction.

"He will face the Swordcraft Club president from Class 3-B—Jean Bael! Jean has won forty-nine out of forty-nine matches! His mastery of the blade and overpowering swordcraft are a sight to behold!"

The announcer moved on to the rules next.

"The rules are simple—it's a one-on-one duel performed with bamboo swords! In the interest of safety, Soul Attire is forbidden!"

Once she finished, the receptionist from before handed me a bamboo sword.

"Are you both ready? On your mark—begin!" the announcer proclaimed.

My duel with Jean Bael, the Swordcraft Club president, began.

■

I held my bamboo sword in front of my navel as soon as the announcer gave the signal, assuming the middle stance. Jean mirrored me, holding his sword in the exact same position.

Jean Bael was tall at about 180 centimeters, and he was wearing the Thousand Blade Academy uniform. He had short black hair and handsome features. He was also wearing silver-rimmed glasses—he must have had vision problems.

He's the president of the Swordcraft Club... I was actually really interested to see his fighting style.

"Allen Rodol. I heard from Sirtie that you rejected her invitation to join our club," Jean said.

"Y-yeah, I guess...," I responded.

Sirtie Rosette was a second-year student who served as the vice president of the Swordcraft Club. She practiced a defensive school of swordcraft called the Open Circle Style. *Can what she did during Recruiting really be called an "invitation," though?*

I had crossed blades with Sirtie during the New Student Recruiting Period in May. *That was when I went to check out the Swordcraft Club with Lia and Rose, if I recall correctly.* Sirtie had blockaded the entrance to the gymnasium and demanded that I give her a match. *That was definitely more of a detainment than an invitation.*

Jean interrupted my trip down memory lane.

"You've refused us once already, but I really would like to have you in the Swordcraft Club."

"...Huh?" I uttered, taken aback by the sudden offer. He continued on.

"Vexingly, we've been reduced to something of a talent incubator for other clubs. We work hard to acquire promising first years, and as soon as we train them to become skilled swordsmen, they get snatched away from us." He grimaced, clenching his fists.

"That's terrible…"

Club budgets were determined by the Club Budget War. A large club like Swordcraft's would have their activity greatly limited if they didn't secure a decent budget. For that reason, the poaching of their promising first years threatened the very survival of the club.

"Who would do something like that?" I asked.

"Only the most evil girl of our time, Student Council President Shii Arkstoria!"

"Th-the president?!"

She would never… Actually, I could totally see it. *Yeah, she would do that without hesitation.* My poker match with her flashed into my mind. I could still remember her kind smile as she nonchalantly cheated by using gimmick cards. You might not have been able to tell by looking at her, but she had a bit of a wicked streak.

"Lilim Chorine and Tirith Magdarote, currently the secretary and treasurer of the Student Council, respectively, were once members of the Swordcraft Club. They were both such brilliant young prospects…," Jean muttered while staring off into the distance.

"Really?" I had never heard that before.

"Yes, they were supposed to carry the Swordcraft Club in the future. That was until that detestable Shii Arkstoria stole them from us. I still don't know how she did it…"

"Huh…"

Now that I thought about it, I remembered Shii saying that she'd recruited them.

"And now this year, she stole *you* from me," Jean said, pointing at me.

Uh, I did enter the Student Council, but the similarities end there. I hadn't planned on joining the Swordcraft Club to begin with, so you couldn't say I was stolen from them.

"I want to make one thing clear: You are headed down the wrong path!" Jean declared.

"U-uh… The wrong path?" I asked.

"I've been doing my research on you, Allen. People say that there's nothing you relish more in the world than blood and violence; that you founded a shady cult called the Practice-Swing Club; that you have an uncontrollable lust for money... You have quite the poor reputation," he said, and calmly shook his head.

"Ah-ha-ha... That really does sound bad...," I responded awkwardly. I had no idea the rumors had gotten *that* out of hand. I needed to find a way to fix this.

"But now that I'm standing opposite you, I've made a realization. You're a pure and honest swordsman at heart."

"U-um... Thank you."

I wasn't sure how to respond, so I simply thanked him.

"Your beautiful middle stance is right out of the textbooks, you know to keep your opponent in the center of your vision, and your posture doesn't give away your center of gravity. You couldn't have gained any of that overnight. I can tell you have spent an enormous amount of time with the blade."

About a billion years, to be precise.

"And now that witch is sullying the beautiful swordcraft you gained from that untiring diligence! I'm going to beat your warped character back into shape!"

As soon as he finished speaking...

"Hiiiiyaaaaaaah!"

He charged directly at me with a spirited cry.

"Fang Chain Style—Decastrike!"

He performed a chain of attacks aimed accurately for my head, chest, abdomen, and other vital points.

"..."

I dodged them easily and recalled my last duel. *Jean definitely isn't slow with the blade. He's actually impressively fast, as you would expect from the president of the Swordcraft Club... As far as I can tell, anyway.* Compared to Idora, however, his agility was a little lacking.

"Tch, you're not bad!" Jean remarked.

After dodging all of his swings, I performed a counterattack.

"Eighth Style—Eight-Span Crow!"

One refined strike became eight separate slashes.

"What the?! Gah..."

All of my slashes connected violently.

"""..."""

The previously raucous crowd fell so silent you could hear a pin drop.

"J-Jean Bael has been defeated! Allen Rodol is the winner! What an overwhelming victory! First years aren't supposed to be able to do that to third years! I'm actually a little scared!"

Having bested the Dojo Challenge, I made to leave the stage.

"Huh?!"

"This...isn't over..." Jean had grabbed the cuff of my pants. "The true Thousand Blade Festival is yet to begin...," he said, before finally losing consciousness.

The "true" Thousand Blade Festival? What did he mean by that? I thought about his last words as I descended from the stage.

"I knew you would crush him, Allen!"

"Looks like your experience at the Sword Master Festival has made you even stronger."

Lia and Rose rejoined me, both wearing proud expressions. I then grabbed the giant hippo doll as the prize for my victory.

"Here you go, Lia. It's the stuffed hippo you wanted," I said, giving her the plushie.

"Thank you, Allen. I'm so happy!" Lia responded.

"I'm glad to hear it."

"I'll treasure it forever!" She beamed with childlike innocence and hugged the stuffed hippo tight. "...Okay, I've decided! Your name is Hippoman!"

Lia wasted no time in giving christening the hippo. I thought she could've picked a better one, but I elected not to comment because I didn't want to dampen her joy.

We resumed exploring the festival and enjoying all the events, and before we knew it, it was five in the evening—closing time for the Thousand Blade Festival. The large number of guests streamed out of the academy, leaving the Thousand Blade students alone to clean up.

The members of Class 1-A shared lively conversation as we took down the decorations in our classroom.

"The hot dogs from that third-year class were stupid good… Man, I really wish I had eaten one more…"

"Did you have one of those chocolate bananas from class 2-F? They were heavenly!"

"The haunted house was terrifying. I thought I was going to have a heart attack…"

We all reflected on the day as we cleaned up. It was fun, but also made me sad that it was all over. We had the classroom back to normal after about an hour, just before a broadcast began over the academy's intercom.

"Ahem, this is Chairwoman Reia Lasnote. Great job today, students! I saw all of the events, and every one of them was amazing! The responses on the visitor surveys were extremely positive. I think we can call this year's Thousand Blade Festival a roaring success! That's the end of the *official* Thousand Blade Festival. Now for the moment you've all been waiting for—the Shadow Thousand Blade Festival! The night's festivities are far from over!"

""""YEEEEEAAAAAAAAHHHHHHHH!!!""""

A roar loud enough to shake the ground rose throughout the building in response to the chairwoman's announcement.

"Sh-Shadow Thousand Blade Festival?"

"What's that? I've never heard of it!"

I remembered something as all my classmates began to talk at once. *This must be the "true" Thousand Blade Festival that Jean mentioned.* The festival apparently wasn't over yet. Actually, it sounded like it was just getting started.

∎

Chairwoman Reia explained the Shadow Thousand Blade Festival and its rules next. The shadow festival was a competition to steal the most "zin," which was a currency used only at the Thousand Blade Festival. Each class was required to divide up the zin they earned during the festival so that each student had at least one thousand. We competed as classes rather than as individuals, and the class with the most zin when time ran out won.

The general public had left the academy, so Soul Attire was allowed. Surprise attacks and mismatched duels were fair game as well—this was an all-out war where anything went. *It's basically combat, with the entire academy as a battleground.*

The class that won the shadow festival received hefty sum of prize money and the title of "Thousand Blade's Strongest."

"That's it for the rules. The Shadow Thousand Blade Festival begins at seven and ends an hour later at eight. The usual bell will signal the beginning and end. Best of luck out there, boys and girls!" the chairwoman said, ending her broadcast.

I saw a fighting spirit burning in the eyes of my classmates after we listened to the broadcast in silence.

"Heh-heh, Thousand Blade really is the best!"

"I had no idea there was such an epic event at the end of the festival!"

"The prize money sounds nice, but I really want the title of 'Thousand Blade's Strongest'!"

Everyone in the class looked fired up and full of motivation.

"We have to win, Allen!"

"We may be first years, but I don't intend to lose!"

Lia and Rose were eager to fight as well.

"Yeah, let's give it our all."

We divided the zin we earned from the cosplay café equally among ourselves and calmly waited for the start of the event.

"Phew…" I let out a large breath to steady my breathing, and Tessa clapped me on the shoulders.

"Yo, Allen. Want to have a little competition to see which of us gets the most zin?" he proposed.

"Sure, that sounds fun," I agreed.

"Heh-heh, that's what I wanna hear!"

We continued to talk until the *ding-dong-ding-dong* of the school bell rang. The Shadow Thousand Blade Festival had begun.

"All right, let's go kick some ass!" Tessa proclaimed. He ran to the door and yanked it open, and was immediately hit square in the stomach by a club made of ice.

"GAAAH!"

""""T-Tessa?!""""

His eyes rolled to the back of his head and he collapsed. That blow had caught him completely unawares. Unfortunately, he would likely be out of it for the remainder of the festival.

"Dammit, who did that?!" I shouted, and dashed out of the classroom. "H-huh?!"

A crowd of upperclassmen had surrounded the Class 1-A classroom. There were over one hundred of them—a union more than four classes large.

"Heh, the best strategy is always to take out the strongest class first!"

"That's right. None of us have a chance until Allen is out of the picture."

"It feels wrong as an upperclassman doing this to a first-year class, but this is a no-holds-barred war!"

They spoke to one another as they each readied their Soul Attire.

I didn't expect them to gang up on us like this right away... Taking on this many upperclassmen at once is going to be really hard, I thought anxiously.

"Conquer—Dragon King Fafnir!"

"Blossom—Winter Sakura!"

In an instant, black and white flames and a brilliant blizzard of cherry blossom petals engulfed the upperclassman.

"Hmm-hmm, trying to take us out right away is smart, but did you really think a paltry one hundred people was going to be enough?" Lia taunted.

"I hope you're ready to taste the steel of my Cherry Blossom Blade Style!" Rose shouted.

They both summoned their Soul Attire and grinned fearlessly.

"Ravage—Storm King!"

"Suck Dry—Immortal Worm!"

"Demolish—Pleasure Doctor!"

Inspired by Lia and Rose, the rest of my classmates summoned their Soul Attire one after another.

...That's right. I don't have to fight alone! I had my friends at my side. That was a reassuring thought.

"Let's do this, Allen!" Lia said.

"Time to show them what we've got!" Rose added.

They both looked at me with determined expressions.

"You bet!"

I enveloped myself in pitch-black darkness and engaged the group of more than one hundred upperclassmen.

■

One hard struggle later, we managed to drive away the assault of the upperclassmen.

"Dammit... You're a monster..."

A student I'd struck with Eight-Span Crow lost consciousness.

"Phew, they sure were strong...," I said to myself. I wiped sweat off my brow and surveyed my surroundings.

"""" """"
...

There were over fifty upperclassmen collapsed on the ground around me. My classmates had taken on the other half of the alliance. *The second and third years are all skilled, but Lia and Rose are with the rest of the class. I'm sure they'll be fine.*

Those two were elite swordswomen. They were likely finishing their opponents off right this moment.

"Guess I should go ahead and take my spoils."

I began opening the wallets of the collapsed students and taking their zin bucks. *This isn't real money, and the rules encourage this, but...* Fishing through the wallets of my unconscious upperclassmen felt wrong.

...That said, the Shadow Thousand Blade Festival is an all-out brawl where everyone represents their class. I couldn't afford to hold my classmates back. I told myself that as I quickly collected the zin.

"That's all of it... I got quite a lot."

I stuffed the huge stacks of bills into the pockets of my uniform. Just as I was about to join up with my classmates, I heard the voices of two girls coming from the hallway.

"Mwa-ha-ha! Hello there, Allen! How're you feeling after fifty people at once?"

"I hate to do this while you're tired, but we would like a match..."

It was Lilim and Tirith.

"...I have to fight you two now, huh?" I responded.

They had both already drawn their blades. Smiles of satisfaction formed on their faces as they eyed my various slash wounds.

"This is perfect! They softened him up for us!" exclaimed Lilim.

"This may not be the honorable thing to do, but we know we can't take you in a fair fight."

It looked like they were planning to profit from the efforts of the last group.

"Hate to break it to you, but I'm feeling just fine," I said.

I focused the darkness onto my injuries and instantly healed them.

""Huh…?!""

Lilim's and Tirith's eyes widened in astonishment.

"W-wow, I didn't know the darkness could heal you… You're mean, Allen. Have you been hiding that from us?" asked Lilim.

"No, I just found out about it myself." I'd discovered the darkness's healing abilities when I fought Idora. It wasn't like I had been intentionally hiding it. "Wanna get started?" I asked with a grin, now completely healed. I took one step toward them, and stopped when they both cried out.

"H-hold on, give us a sec!"

"W-we're not ready…!"

They began to confer in a whisper.

"Wh-what should we do, Tirith…? We can't beat Allen if he isn't injured!"

"Honestly, I think it's hopeless. Shii will never let us hear the end of it if we withdraw here, though…"

"…Well, Allen's darkness isn't infinite. Do you think we could drain him of spirit power if we avoid close combat and attack mainly from long-distance?"

"I have bad news for you there. Allen has more spirit power than Black Fist…"

"…Is he invincible? Does he have a single flaw?"

Lilim and Tirith glanced at me repeatedly as they talked, their faces growing pale all the while. *I have no idea what they're talking about, but I want to get this over with…* Other upperclassmen would find us if we dawdled here too long.

"I don't mind making the first move if you're just going to stand there," I announced, drawing my sword and taking another step forward.

"Crap, it's do-or-die, Tirith! Let's show him what second years are made of!" Lilim yelled.

"I'm going to attack, so focus on holding him in place!" Tirith ordered.

They produced their Soul Attire simultaneously, and a grand battle began.

■

My duel with Lilim and Tirith was cutthroat. They avoided engaging me head-on, instead insisting on attacking me mainly from long range. I struggled with long-range opponents, and on top of that, they knew all my moves. That naturally made for a tough fight.

But at the end of the intense duel, I somehow managed to best them.

"Geez... Th-that was impressive...," Lilim gasped.

"You were too strong for us... after all...," Tirith mumbled.

"Haah, haah...," I panted.

They had me at a numbers disadvantage, but even discounting that, they were both really good. The two girls covered for each other with perfect coordination and remained committed to their long-distance attacks. They'd been desperate to win, and they had an excellent strategy.

...I need to find somewhere to rest. I took out fifty students and followed that up with an intense battle with Lilim and Tirith. *I overdid it a little with the darkness...* I still had energy to spare, but I could get roped into another engagement at any moment. I needed to rest while I could.

Where would be the best place to hide...? That would work. I decided on a hiding place, swiped the zin bucks out of Lilim's and Tirith's wallets, and quietly got moving. Taking care to avoid the eyes of the upperclassmen, I snuck my way to the Student Council room. It was located some distance from the rest of the classrooms, and I doubted anyone would go that far out of their way while the shadow festival was in full swing.

"Phew, I can finally take a breather...," I said with a sigh of relief after I entered the room. I then heard a voice.

"Welcome, Allen."

It was Shii Arkstoria.

"Huh?!"

She walked toward me with a bewitching smile, lit by the moonlight coming through the windows.

"P-President… What are you doing here?!"

"Hmm-hmm, did I surprise you? You fought Lilim and Tirith right after taking out a large alliance of second and third years. I figured you would come here to rest up from your exhaustion," she explained.

"Oh… You must have been the one who convinced the upperclassmen to attack us in the first place," I realized.

"My, whatever are you talking about?" she said with a kind smile, playing dumb.

I bet she isn't denying it outright because she never directly asked them to do it. The president was very cunning. She'd probably used her silver tongue to manipulate the second and third years into joining up and attacking Class 1-A.

Well, I can't blame her for that. Anything went in the Shadow Thousand Blade Festival. The ability to manipulate people with words was a powerful weapon to have at your disposal.

One thing worried me, though.

"Can I ask you one question?" I asked.

"Sure, what is it?" she responded.

"Have you, uh…been waiting here this entire time?"

Close to fifty minutes had already passed since the shadow festival began. It was nearing eight at night in the middle of September, and our uniforms weren't the best protection against the cold. She must have been freezing if she had been waiting motionlessly in this room all this time without even turning on the lights.

"Y-yeah, I have! Do you have a problem with… A-achoo!"

With perfect timing, Shii sneezed like a cute little animal.

"…President. Please think before you act—"

"You have no business lecturing your elder!" Shii interrupted, blushing and pounding her fist on a desk.

For how mean-spirited she can be, she can also be quite the airhead. She was like a mischievous little devil you just couldn't bring yourself to hate.

"You look like you're not feeling so good, so would you be willing to let me go?" I asked.

"Don't count on it!" she shouted, refusing the lifeline I gave her completely. That's about what I expected.

"A fight is only going to make you feel worse, though… You'll regret it later," I said, once again politely refusing her. She responded with a boastful smile.

"Hmm-hmm, I think there's a misunderstanding here."

"What would that be?"

"We are going to fight, but I never said it was going to be a sword fight."

"…Oh no." I had a bad feeling about this. This was feeling very similar to what happened in this room a few months back.

"I don't think for a second that I can beat you in a one-on-one sword fight. So this is what we're going to do instead!" she exclaimed, producing a pack of cards from her pocket and setting it on a desk.

I knew it. The president was a sore loser, and she still hadn't gotten over her last defeat. I stared at the cards unenthusiastically.

"Are those trick cards again?" I asked.

"Ha, don't insult me. Do you really think I would use the same tactics twice?" she denied, unreservedly handing me the deck of cards. I examined them closely.

"…These are definitely ordinary cards," I said. There were no gimmicks like last time. It was a perfectly normal deck. "Are you okay with poker for the game?"

"Yes, of course. I do have one proposal—how about we change the dealer after each game?"

"Huh…"

The president was essentially challenging me to a cheating contest. She had probably been honing her sham abilities ever since her last defeat. I saw a strong confidence in her eyes.

"That's fine with me. Let's play." I grinned, competitive spirit burning within me.

Ol' Bamboo had taught me a great many games, including mahjong, roulette, and Cee-lo. He'd explained not only the rules and useful tactics, but also common methods of cheating, along with how to foil them. Of all the games I knew, I was best at card games. I was so good that Ol' Bamboo even said that he had nothing left to teach me.

I glanced at my watch and saw that it was ten minutes to eight. There were ten minutes until end of the shadow festival, so this would likely be my last match.

"Hmm-hmm, shall we begin?" Shii asked.

"You're on," I responded.

And so the president and I began a quiet kind of duel in the Student Council room.

■

Shii's ambush led to our first poker match in three months. We sat on opposite sides of a desk.

"We're going by regular poker rules. No funny business. Whoever gets three wins first is the victor. The dealer will change after each game. Any questions?" she asked.

"No, I'm good," I nodded.

She offered me the deck of cards. "Hmm-hmm, I give you the first deal."

"Are you sure?"

"Yes. You accepted all of my terms, so it's only fair."

"Okay. I will."

I took the deck, shuffled it three times, and dealt us five cards each.

"Hmm, I'll exchange one card," she said.

"Here you go," I responded, granting her request.

"Thanks."

She grinned slightly when she saw her new card. It seemed like she liked what she had.

"I'm ready to play my hand. How many are you going to swap?" Shii asked. She put her cards facedown on the table and smiled confidently.

"Actually, I'm going to play my hand as is," I answered with a smile, not even looking at my hand once.

"H-huh… You sure are confident." The president looked shaken for a moment, but quickly recovered and revealed her hand. "I have a flush of diamonds! Let's see your hand!"

"All right."

I flipped over my cards one by one.

Ten of spades. Jack of spades. Queen of spades. King of spades.

"What the heck?!"

And the final card—ace of spades.

"Wow, would you look at that… It's a royal straight flush," I said.

I'd won the first match. I was off to a good start.

"Y-you sure wasted no time… How in the world did you do that?" she demanded.

"Ah-ha-ha, it was just luck," I answered, feigning ignorance while performing three quick riffle shuffles.

"…?!"

Shii's face had gone pale. Guess that was an understandable reaction.

I calmly handed her the deck of cards.

"Here you go. It's your turn to deal next."

"Allen… How…?"

She glared at me and accepted the deck with trembling hands.

"Is something wrong?" I asked.

"No, it's nothing…" She bit her lip in clear frustration as she dealt the cards, and our second game began.

I looked at my five cards. I had a two, a three, a four, a and a pair of sevens. *I've got twin sevens. A straight wouldn't be impossible, but… going for three of a kind is the smart play.*

I had already foiled Shii's trick, and I had two turns left as the dealer. This wasn't the time to take risks.

"I'll exchange three cards, please," I requested.

"…Sure, here you are," she responded.

I discarded the two, the three, and the four, and accepted three new cards. My hand now was seven-seven-seven-eight-ten; I had three of a kind. *Okay, that's not bad.* The odds of getting three of a kind in a random hand of five was about two percent. This was a very strong hand in a game of poker with only one card exchange. In a normal game with no cheating, this would almost always win.

The president swapped a card, and we revealed our hands together.

I had three of a kind with sevens, and she had two pairs with two twos and two eights. That meant I won.

"Looks like luck is on my side today," I said.

" . . . "

Shii looked visibly upset over how badly her plan was being derailed.

"Shall we move on to the next game?" I asked, reaching for the deck.

"H-hold on!" she cried.

"What is it?"

"Tell me you how you got that royal straight flush in the first game! I need to know!"

The president was still caught up in trying to figure out how I cheated. She'd probably sensed that she was going to lose unless she did something.

"I didn't *do* anything," I answered honestly.

"Grr... You've got guts lying to the Student Council president like that!" she seethed. She stood up with a huff and stomped toward me. "Roll them up."

"Huh?"

"Roll up your sleeves! I remember you hid your cards inside them last time!"

"O-okay..."

Not feeling like I had any choice, I did as Shii demanded and rolled up my sleeves. She patted down my arms to see if I was hiding cards anywhere.

"Huh... You really don't have any."

"Like I've been saying, I really didn't do anything..."

"L-like I'd believe that! You have to be hiding cards somewhere... Ah, maybe around your chest!"

"How would I make that work?"

It would be extremely difficult to pull cards from my chest area without her noticing.

"I-I don't... Don't bother resisting!" she shouted, then searched my chest area, my stomach area, and even reached her hands into my pants pockets to make absolutely sure I wasn't hiding any cards. But I didn't have any. She wasn't going to find what I didn't have.

"Um, are you satisfied?" I asked.

"Th-that's... Did that really happen by chance? No, that's ridiculous...

A royal straight flush is a hand you'd be lucky to get once in your life…," she muttered, pale-faced.

"Sorry, but can I roll up my sleeves? I'm getting kind of cold."

"Absolutely not! You'll cheat the moment I take my eyes off you!"

"B-but, President…you just searched me and didn't find anything," I said with an awkward smile and a small sigh.

"…Oh! I get it now! You're not hiding cards—you've messed with the deck somehow!" she accused, looking at the cards on the desk. "I don't know how you did it, but I know just what to do!"

Shii feverishly shuffled the cards and cut the deck multiple times.

"Ha-ha-ha… That should foil whatever you did! Not even you could cheat now!" she exclaimed, pointing at me with a triumphant expression.

"O-okay… Can I deal now?"

"Certainly. The real battle starts now!"

"…I guess so."

I gave her the stink eye and quickly shuffled the deck. I dealt us five cards each, and Shii exchanged two cards.

"Yes!" she squeaked happily, pumping her fist. She must have gotten a good hand.

"Okay, should we reveal our hands?" I asked. Her face stiffened.

"U-uh, Allen… Are you not going to swap any cards?"

"Yeah, I want to play this hand."

"But you haven't even looked at it. Just like last time…"

Her voice trembled. This must have brought back bad memories of our first match.

"Ah-ha-ha. I like leaving it all to luck in big showdowns like this."

"R-really… Fine, let's do it! I have a full house! Beat that!"

"Let's see what I've got…"

Starting from the right, I turned over my cards one by one. The first card was the ten of spades.

"O-oh come on…" Shii went speechless as déjà vu struck.

The rest of the cards appeared in the exact same order as before. Jack of spades. Queen of spades. King of spades. And the final card—ace of spades, of course.

"Wow, I have a royal straight flush again. I can't even begin to imagine the odds of that," I said.

"I-I lost...?" Shii muttered in despair.

I won in three games. Our rematch ended in my overwhelming victory.

■

I started to clean up the cards on the desk after winning my showdown with the president.

"Wh-what...? That's not...," Shii mumbled, her voice trembling.

Disbelief was written on her face. She couldn't have seen this coming in her wildest dreams. *Well, that's a natural reaction...* After all, she'd prepared three different methods of cheating for our match.

First, she'd stacked the deck. I noticed it when I examined the deck to see if they were trick cards. *She must have been really confident I wouldn't see what she did.* The ruse was plainly obvious if you had any experience cheating at cards: she had arranged them in increments of three—one, four, seven, ten, king, and so on.

This is a typical method used to prevent your opponent from getting a good hand. With the cards arranged in skips of three, it was difficult to even get one pair, let alone something better like a straight.

Allowing me to deal first was also part of her plan. She'd sneaked out the cards that emerged in the first game that could form pairs and slipped them onto the bottom of the deck.

She had also resorted to two other methods of cheating: a false shuffle, where you shuffle the cards without actually changing the order at all, and the bottom deal, where you deal yourself cards from the bottom while making it look like you're dealing them from the top.

She probably practiced really hard for this day... The president had performed both of those two tricks at a very high level. Stacking the deck to make getting a good hand difficult could have been enough for her to win, but she'd combined that with the false shuffle and bottom deal to ensure that she would always beat one pair.

It was a simple strategy, but a very effective one with a low risk of failure. If I hadn't done anything, she would have won nine times out of ten. However, it only took one move to easily foil her plan—the riffle shuffle. The way she stacked the deck is effective against ordinary methods of shuffling that don't change the order of the cards all that much. It has no chance against the riffle shuffle, though, which randomizes a deck much more efficiently.

The president had done her best to hold on with the false shuffle and bottom deal, but her plan was built around stacking the deck, and there was nothing she could do once I foiled that.

"I won, President. Can I please have your zin now?" I asked firmly, seeking my reward as the victor in our contest of cheating.

"H-hold on!" she responded. She wasn't giving them to me... Why was I not surprised? "How did you cheat?! I won't get mad if you just fess up right now!"

"Well, like I said, I didn't really do anything that could be called cheating."

"You liar! Getting two royal straight flushes in a row is absolutely impossible!"

She was clearly convinced that I'd conned her.

"Ah-ha-ha... I'd rather not answer that. Can you just let this go?"

There was no benefit to revealing your tricks. Besides, I hadn't *technically* cheated. It would be more appropriate to call it skill.

"No way! I won't give you my zin until you tell me what you did!" Shii yelled, huffing like a child.

"*Haah*... I see." I sighed. I stood up from my chair and inspected her clothes. *I don't see any bulges... I doubt she has much zin.* That meant it wouldn't be a huge deal if I didn't collect hers.

"Wh-why'd you fall silent? And why are you staring at me like that?!" she shouted, crossing her arms in front of her chest and stepping back. Her cheeks were flushed slightly, and her eyes were moist.

"Don't worry about it. I'll see you later," I answered, turning to leave the Student Council room.

"W-wait...!" she shouted.

"What is it?" I asked.

"I-I'm begging you, please tell me how you cheated! I won't be able to sleep tonight if you leave me like this!" the president pleaded desperately, grabbing my hands.

"I don't know..."

I really had nothing to gain by telling her how I did it.

"I-if you don't tell me, I'll..."

"...Yeah?"

"I'll tell everyone that you groped me!" she yelled, blushing furiously. I couldn't believe what she'd said.

"...Please don't do that," I asked.

I was already stressed about the terrible rumors circulating about me. If word spread that I'd violated a member of House Arkstoria, there was a chance the holy knights would get involved.

"S-so, which will you choose? Do you want to do the right thing and reveal how you cheated, or have a rumor spread that you...that you touched me? You can only pick one!" she yelled, blushing and leaning her face into mine. I caught a whiff of her sweet girly scent and felt my pulse quicken.

"*Haah*, guess I have no choice." I sighed, giving in.

"Yes! I knew you would choose correctly!" Shii rejoiced, clapping her hands and smiling with childlike innocence.

"All right, name a hand that's difficult to get. Anything will work," I requested.

"Hmm... What about a straight?" she responded.

"Ah-ha-ha, that's too easy."

I quickly shuffled the deck and dealt the top five cards.

"...What are you doing?"

"Can you flip them over for me?"

"S-sure... Huh?! It's a straight!" she shouted, astonished. "H-how the heck did you do that?!"

"I didn't do anything complicated. Let's see... Do you know how people count cards in blackjack?" I inquired.

"Y-yes... It's a method of keeping track of how many cards with a value of ten or more are left in the deck, making it less likely you will bust by going over twenty-one points...right?" Shii answered unconfidently.

"Good job, that's mostly right. What I'm doing is an advanced form of that—I'm memorizing the deck," I revealed.

"Memorizing the deck? What do you mean?"

"Just that. I memorize the order of all the cards in the deck, which is fifty-two cards including all the numbers and suits."

"That has to be impossible!"

"It's actually pretty simple once you get used to it. It's not half as hard as learning the multiplication table."

"But…even if that's possible, wouldn't it be rendered pointless once you shuffle?!"

"Not if you watch closely. All you have to do is change the order of the cards in your head as you shuffle."

Compared to an all-out sword fight where less than a second could mean your life, following the movement of cards as they were shuffled wasn't so hard. If you could do that, all you needed to do next was reorder the cards in your head each time they were shuffled.

"Once you've memorized the order of the deck, the game is as good as yours. You just shuffle so that the cards you want end up on top and… voilà."

I dealt five cards in front of Shii, and she flipped them over. Her jaw dropped.

"…"

It was a royal straight flush, just like I gave myself multiple times earlier.

"Wh-what…? This means it's impossible to beat you if you're the dealer!" she exclaimed, glaring at me.

"That's not necessarily the case. It's only thanks to you I was able to memorize the cards this time," I objected.

"Huh?"

"Memorizing the order of fifty-two cards instantaneously is not possible, no matter how good you are. You need a decent amount of time to study them."

"Then when did you…? Oh no! Did you do it then?!"

"Yes, it was when you allowed me to investigate the cards. I pretended that I was checking to see if they were trick cards, while actually memorizing the deck."

It actually wouldn't have mattered if they were trick cards or not. My victory was guaranteed once I memorized the deck.

"I-I can't believe it... That means I never stood a chance..."

"Yes, my victory was guaranteed from the beginning."

That was the end of my explanation.

"...Allen. If you can manipulate the order of the deck freely, were you messing with me in that final game?" the president asked. She picked up on that immediately... Nothing got by her.

"Wh-what do you mean...?" I had a feeling I knew what she was talking about, but I played dumb on the small hope I could get out of it.

"I got a full house in the last game, and I was so happy. I was all like, 'Yes, I can beat Allen with this hand!' But hearing your explanation made me realize something... You set that hand up, didn't you?" she accused, glaring at me.

...There was no escaping this.

"Ah-ha-ha... Sorry, I thought it would be fun to mess with you a bit. I wanted to see your reaction...," I confessed.

I'd done it on a total whim. She was being so expressive throughout the match, and I was having so much fun watching her that I couldn't help myself.

"I-I knew it! ...Fine. This is what I do to mean boys like you!" Shii proclaimed, jumping up from her chair and walking to a large window behind her. She opened the window with a practiced hand. "HEEEEEEEY! ALLEN IS OVER HERE! HE'S ALL ROUGHED UP, SO NOW'S YOUR BEST CHANCE!" she yelled for everyone to hear, giving away my hiding place.

"P-President?!"

"Hmph! I'll have nothing to do with a kid who bullies his elder! ... Achoo!"

"Good grief... I'm leaving! Also, keep warm tonight so you don't catch a cold!" I rushed to say before fleeing the classroom. I didn't get far.

""""We've found you, Allen Rodol!""""

Three upperclassmen were waiting for me. They must have been nearby when Shii announced my location. The group grew in size until I was completely surrounded.

"Heh-heh, you really are beaten up!"

"Sorry, but we can't let a first-year class win the grand prize!"

"Don't hold this against us, okay? Anything goes in the shadow festival."

They were all smiling confidently, inching toward me with Soul Attire manifested

Crap, I have nowhere to run... There can't be more than a few minutes left before the end of the festival. I could last for a few minutes!

"...You've got me cornered. Let's make this last bout one to remember!" I said, pouring what little spirit power I had remaining into my body and engulfing the surrounding area with pitch-black darkness.

"Wh-what's this?!"

"Do you live under a rock? We saw this at the Sword Master Festival! This darkness is his power!"

"Be vigilant! We still don't know what kind of ability it is!"

The darkness set my upperclassmen on edge.

"Are you all ready?"

I fought my heart out until the final bell rang for the end of the Shadow Thousand Blade Festival.

■

Once the intense skirmish came to an end, I dragged my tired body back to the 1-A classroom. I opened the door.

"A-Allen! Thank goodness you're okay!"

"Not even all those upperclassmen could defeat you... You're truly amazing."

Lia and Rose rushed toward me, both of them wrapped in bandages.

"Yeah, I got through it somehow. Are you two okay?" I asked.

"Yeah, this is nothing!" Lia exclaimed.

"These are just scratches. I'm fine," Rose assured me.

"That's good to hear."

The rest of the class gathered around us as we talked.

"Yo, Allen. How much zin did you rack up?"

"Let's see which of us got more!"

Everyone really wanted to know how much zin I had.

"I haven't counted yet, but I think I got quite a lot," I announced, and pulled out the massive amount of zin bucks I had stuffed in my various pockets.

"Holy crap!"

"This is by far the most in the class... No, make that the whole academy..."

Dry laughter filled the room until the door crashed open to reveal Chairwoman Reia holding a large box.

"Hey kids, great job today! I'm here to collect your zin... Wow! That's a ton! You all might win!" she said before shoving all the zin into her box and leaving for a different class.

We passed the time talking excitedly about things like the strongest opponents we faced, what kind of Soul Attire we saw, and more until an announcement began over the intercom.

"Good evening, boys and girls! That was the best Thousand Blade Festival we've had in some time, both the official and the shadow! I won't keep you waiting any longer—let's get right to the results! The winner of this year's Shadow Thousand Blade Festival is... Class 1-A in a landslide!"

The class immediately erupted in cheer.

""""YEEEEAAAAAAHHHHH!""""

"We did it! That means we get the title of Thousand Blade's Strongest, right?!"

"Yeah, we're the best in name and reality!"

"Don't we get a bunch of prize money, too?! That's so exciting! How should we use it?!"

Everyone was thrilled by our victory, and we ended up deciding to hold a party to celebrate both it and the end of the festival.

"A celebration party...are you two going?" I asked Lia and Rose.

"Hmm... I'll go if you go," Lia answered.

"I don't mind either way," Rose said.

"Well, it would be a shame to miss it... Let's go!"

"Okay!"

"Sure."

I went to the party with Lia and Rose, and had a blast talking with them late into the night.

CHAPTER 3

The Five Powers &
The Thirteen Oracle Knights

It was the day after the Thousand Blade Festival, and Lia and I were walking to the 1-A classroom.

""*Hraah...*""

On the way there, Lia and I yawned at almost the exact same time.

"Ah-ha-ha, that was a really big yawn," I teased.

"Hmm-hmm, right back at you," Lia giggled.

We'd both stayed out late at the party, so neither of us got enough sleep.

"It's a little cold today...," I said. The sky was blanketed by clouds. They were dark and thick, and it looked like it could start raining at any moment.

"It really is. I think we start wearing our winter uniforms on October first?" she mused.

We continued to talk until we reached the main school building. I opened the classroom door, and was greeted by a rare sight. Rose, who everyone knew as a terrible morning person, was already in her seat. *Rose getting here this early... I've really seen it all now.*

Lia and I put down our stuff at our desks and greeted Rose.

"Good morning, Rose," I said.

"Morning, Rose. You're here early," Lia added.

"Hm? Yeah... Good morning. *Hraah*...," she responded, turning toward us with an adorable yawn. Her bedhead was a piece of art, as per usual.

"Ah-ha-ha, you look really tired," I commented.

"Did you have trouble falling asleep last night?" asked Lia.

"*Ngh*, yeah... The party went late last night, and I really overdid it with Winter Sakura... That drained almost all of my spirit power. *Hraah...*" She yawned again, right as the door opened to reveal an elderly male teacher.

Who's that...?

He walked to the teacher's podium and cleared his throat.

"Uh... I have an announcement for you. Uh... The chairwoman left for Liengard Palace this morning after receiving an urgent summons from the government," he said.

All my classmates began talking at once.

"An urgent summons from the government...?"

"Hey, given the timing, think this could be about *them*? You know, the Black Organization?"

"Oh, that would make sense... They could be discussing security measures."

The elderly teacher pulled a sheet of paper out of his pocket.

"Uh... This is a note from the chairwoman. 'Hello, class. I apologize, but due to a sudden matter I am giving you the day for self-study. I've reserved the Soul Attire Room during the morning and afternoon periods, so use it well. Remember, you are not allowed to perform Soul Attire training or use the soul-crystal swords without my supervision. That is all.' And that's what it says. Have a good day."

The teacher bowed deeply and left the classroom.

"Self-study... That's a first for me at Thousand Blade," I said to myself. My days at Grand Swordcraft Academy had essentially consisted of nothing but self-study, so this was kind of nostalgic.

We headed to the Soul Attire Room when the first bell rang, and spent the time studying as each of us pleased. Lia read a swordcraft instruction book, Rose reviewed her Cherry Blossom Blade forms, and Tessa meditated in a corner of the room.

I, meanwhile, performed practice swings in silence. "Ha! Ya! Ho!" Each time I assumed the middle stance, calmly brandished my blade, and swung. It was plain and simple training, but there was nothing more effective. A swordfighter's skill was determined by how many times they'd swung their blade—that was what was written in sword-craft instruction books.

I spent the entire three hours allotted to us this morning swinging my blade without rest.

■

When our lunch break arrived after morning classes, Lia, Rose, and I walked to the Student Council room to attend the regular meeting. I knocked on the door three times, and the president responded like always.

"Good morning," I said as I opened the door and walked in.

"Good morning, Lia and Rose! ...Hello, Allen."

Shii cheerfully greeted Lia and Rose, but greeted me coldly.

"Ah-ha-ha... Are you still angry?" I asked.

"I will not respond to a boy who bullies his elder," she said, looking away.

She's acting more like a whiny kid than a mature elder, I thought, smiling awkwardly.

"...? What are you talking about?" Lia asked in confusion.

"Oh, we played poker yesterday and—"

"Allen touched me," Shii interrupted with a horrifying accusation.

"P-President?! Don't be ridiculous!" I panicked, demanding that she set the record straight.

"...Allen, is that true?" Lia asked.

"...You'd better explain yourself. That's beyond messed up," Rose said.

The light had left their eyes completely, and there was no trace of their usual kind demeanor. They simply stared at me, their faces the definition of blank.

"O-of course it's not true! She's making a bad joke!" Feeling danger to my person, I turned to the president. "A-anyway, enough with the false accusations! We should be even after what you did at the end of the festival, right?!"

She'd sicced a large number of upperclassmen on me as revenge for my little trick. That should have made us even.

"But Allen, you defeated that entire group of students all by your-self... That doesn't feel like revenge at all!" she pouted.

"That's hardly fair...," I protested. I'd defeated them all, sure, but it took almost everything I had. That absolutely should have been good enough for her.

"Hmm... Do you promise to obey me next time?" she asked.

"...Fine. But only if it's a reasonable request," I stipulated.

I couldn't promise to do *anything* she asked me to. I wasn't about to go chasing after a blood diamond like the vice president.

"That works for me. All right, we're friends again," the president said with a wide grin.

...What in the world is she going to ask me to do? Just thinking about it upset my stomach.

"*Haah*... I need to clear up the misunderstanding with Lia and Rose, so can you please just eat lunch in silence, President?" I asked.

"You got it," she responded.

I then gave a thorough explanation of what happened the previous night.

"So that's what happened... Thank goodness...," Lia said.

"Geez, that scared me...," Rose added.

Relief came over their faces and the light returned to their eyes. With that settled, we finally started our lunch meeting.

"Oh yeah... Where are Lilim and Tirith?" Lia asked, looking around as she opened her lunch.

"They're recovering from fatigue. Allen apparently gave them the beating of a lifetime yesterday, and they might not get up for two or three days," Shii explained.

"Ah-ha-ha, I feel kind of bad about that...," I said, laughing awkwardly.

Lilim and Tirith had kept getting back up no matter how many times I knocked them down. Lilim was especially persistent. I didn't think she would ever give in, constantly yelling things like "I'll never lose to a first year!" I'd ended up using a lot of the darkness as a result, which led to me getting ambushed by the president after deciding I needed a rest.

"Don't worry about it. Lilim and Tirith are both strong, so they'll be fine," Shii said. "By the way, what did you think of the haunted house?"

We spent some time talking about the Thousand Blade Festival. We touched on a variety of topics, including how the haunted house could be upgraded for next year's festival; Jean Bael, the president of the Swordcraft Club; and strategy for winning the shadow festival. Once we had nothing left to say about the festival, I changed the topic.

"Oh yeah, Chairwoman Reia isn't here today. We were told she received an urgent summons from the government. Do you know anything about that, President?"

I had been wondering about that since this morning.

"I do. There was an urgent Elite Five Academy Chair Meeting called today. I think my dad said he's participating, too," Shii responded in between bites of her fried egg.

"It's about the Black Organization, isn't it?" I asked.

"That's right. The government has more than had their hands full with them. They've been causing trouble all over the continent. One day they're making a move in Vesteria, then before you know it they're starting things here! There's a rumor that they've been especially fixated on the Principality of Theresia lately," the president ranted. As a member of House Arkstoria, one of the leading political families of Liengard, she must have despised the Black Organization. "There's something else we just learned. The Black Organization is reportedly searching for a rare monster called an eidolon."

Lia's hands froze.

"...What is it, Lia? Did something get stuck in your throat?" I asked, offering her a glass of water.

"H-huh...? Oh, no. I'm fine," she said with an awkward smile, shaking her head.

"Really? That's good."

"Thanks."

Rose spoke up next. "If all of the Elite Five Academy chairs have left for an emergency meeting, is the city properly defended?"

That was a good question. The five chairs all possessed significant authority and strength. It wasn't hard to imagine that the city might be in danger if they all left it at once.

"Hmm, it definitely leaves us a little shorthanded, but... Eh, there's no need to worry. The date for the emergency meeting is top secret. That information will not leak, so there's absolutely no chance the Black Organization will know to attack—"

The president was interrupted by the sound of a massive explosion.

""""Huh?!""""

We hurriedly looked out the window and saw that the gymnasium was on fire. That wasn't all—droves of people in black garb were streaming over the academy's outer wall.

"Th-the Black Organization?!" Shii shouted. A broadcast began over the academy's speakers a moment later.

"Emergency alert! Emergency alert! The academy is under attack from a group believed to be the Black Organization! We ask that all students do their best to intercept! I repeat: the academy..."

The surprise attack immediately threw Thousand Blade into chaos.

"Allen, Lia, Rose. Can I count on your assistance?" Shii asked.

"Of course!"

"Yes!"

"You bet."

We sprinted out of the classroom to meet the Black Organization's assault.

■

With the academy under sudden attack, we headed to the staff room to get a proper grasp on the current situation. The president and Rose were the most experienced of the group, and they calmly decided that acting without a plan would only make things worse.

"Pardon the intrusion," Shii said quickly as we walked through the door.

"Oh, it's Lady Arkstoria! And Allen, too!"

"W-we're saved... Our brains and brawn have arrived!"

The teachers all showed great relief upon our entrance. *The president sure lives up to her family name.* It looked like even the teachers held great trust in her.

As I thought that, Shii walked briskly into the room and addressed a male teacher. He was the deputy chairman, if I recalled correctly.

"Can you please fill me in on the current situation?" she asked.

"Y-yes, ma'am. We have been invaded by roughly three hundred swordsmen wearing black overcoats. We believe they are the Black Organization! They are currently laying siege to the main school building, and we have a force of students primarily from the disciplinary committee and the Swordcraft Club engaging them as we speak!" the deputy chairman informed her.

"I see... How is the fight going?" she inquired.

"...Not well. They are only barely holding them out of the building," he said gravely, and a heavy mood overcame the room.

"Got it. Have you already contacted the holy knights and the chairwoman?"

"Well... We have called them both many times, but we haven't been able to reach them."

"...? What do you mean by that?"

"It seems like the assailants have cut us off from the outside world by placing some kind of barrier around the academy."

The deputy chairman pointed out the window. I strained my eyes, and sure enough, a clear, thin hemisphere was draped over the academy.

"I see it. I wonder if that's from a magic tool or a Soul Attire ability... Either way, that's a problem," the president said after the deputy chairman finished his account of the sticky situation. "Allen, do you think you can break that barrier?" she asked, looking straight at me.

"Me...?" I responded.

"Yes, you. Broadly speaking, there are two ways to take down a barrier: either find and take out the magic tool or sorcerer casting it...or destroy the barrier itself with overpowering strength. We don't know where the source is, so destroying the barrier is our only option. And you, Allen, are the strongest person at this academy," she explained, her expression turning serious. "This barrier is strong enough to cut us off completely from the outside world. I'm also positive that it obstructs recognition of what is happening inside it, meaning we can't expect any support from the outside world. Only members of the Black Organization will be entering the academy. We'll be done for if we don't destroy the barrier as soon as possible."

"...This is a really big responsibility," I said. If I failed to break the barrier, we would be trapped under siege with no hope of reinforcements.

"Sorry, but you're the only one we can ask this of right now," Shii stated, and all eyes in the room turned to me.

"...Okay. I'll give it my best shot."

I couldn't know for sure, but I thought I could do it. I doubted there was any barrier that World Render, the attack I'd used to tear through the Prison of Time, couldn't cut through.

"Thank you, Allen. I knew you would say that. Could you accompany him, Lia and Rose? The enemy isn't stupid—they won't just sit back and watch as he approaches the barrier," Shii requested.

"N-no problem!"

"Roger that."

Lia and Rose agreed without hesitation.

"President, what do you plan on doing?" I asked.

"I'm going to help maintain our line of defense. There will be no recovery if we let them into the main school building," she answered, and then immediately started giving orders to the teachers. "I want a few of you to remain here as liaisons, and the rest of you to join the front lines. The liaisons are to contact the holy knights and the chairwoman as soon as Allen breaks the barrier."

"""Yes, ma'am!"""

The teachers sprang to action.

"I leave the barrier to you, Allen!" Shii said before leading most of the teachers out of the staff room.

It's times like this that her upbringing and intelligence as a member of House Arkstoria really shine. She was normally a careless person, but she was reliable when she needed to be.

"Come on, Allen!" Lia urged.

"We were given the most important job of all. We need to stay focused!" Rose said.

"Yeah, let's go!" I responded.

I flew out of the staff room with Lia and Rose to accomplish our mission.

■

We raced toward the barrier as fast as we could. World Render was tremendously powerful, but its range was limited. I would need to be right next to the barrier to destroy it.

"All right, this passage is clear. Let's go," Rose informed us. She was used to combat situations like this, so we were following her lead.

Breaking the barrier was our top priority. Fighting off the Black Organization would have to wait. As such, we were sneaking through the academy and doing our best to avoid combat.

It was when we were hiding in the shadow of a building that a chill ran down my back.

"Get back, Lia!" I shouted.

"Huh... AAAH?!" Lia screamed.

I shoved Lia into the sunlight on a split-second decision, just before seven slash attacks emerged from the shadow. I drew my sword instantly and managed to deflect six of the slashes, but one got through due to the surprise nature of the attack and sliced me on the left arm.

"Ngh..."

"A-Allen...?! Sorry, are you okay?!" Lia rushed toward me, pale in the face.

"Don't worry, this is nothing," I responded. I concentrated the darkness onto the wound and healed it right away.

"I recognize this shadow-manipulating power... Show yourself, Dodriel!" I yelled.

A boy shimmered into existence like a heat haze out of a perfectly ordinary shadow. His horribly damaged blue hair was tied in the back, and a slash wound ran across his otherwise handsome face. It was

Dodriel Barton—a prodigy from my time at Grand Swordcraft Academy, and now a dweller of darkness who had fallen so low as to join the Black Organization.

"Ah-ha-ha-ha! I'm impressed you spotted that attack... Though I guess I shouldn't be surprised. After all, our hearts are bound by passionate love! Isn't that right, Allen?" he said, laughing like a broken man. His words were as nonsensical as ever.

"You were at the Unity Festival!" Lia exclaimed.

"Yeah, he's the swordsman with that strange Soul Attire...," Rose said.

They both immediately drew their swords and stepped toward Dodriel.

"Go on ahead, Allen! We'll take care of him!" Lia urged.

"Breaking the barrier is top priority. Don't worry about us—we'll catch up in no time," Rose said.

"..."

I hesitated. *Crap, what should I do?!* I was torn between two decisions: stay and fight Dodriel as a group of three or leave him to them and prioritize breaking the barrier.

He defeated Lia and Rose last time... But they were now both significantly stronger than they'd been then. They also already knew what his Soul Attire, Shadow Sovereign, was capable of.

...This is far from the only battle going on here. Blood was running all throughout Thousand Blade at this very moment. The damage would be much worse if I let Dodriel slow me down. Doing as Lia and Rose said and prioritizing the barrier was the correct tactical choice.

"...Fine. I've told you this before, but Dodriel can enter the Shadow World. You may outnumber him and know his ability, but don't take him lightly!" I warned.

"Okay!"

"Ha, don't worry about us!"

"Good luck!" I said, and sprinted toward the barrier.

"Huh?! Are you leaving me, Allen?!" Dodriel cried out in sorrow.

"Turn around, buster," Lia said.

"You're ours!" Rose proclaimed.

I then heard the clash of steel on steel. *Lia, Rose…I'll come back as soon as I break the barrier.*

I cloaked my legs in pitch-black darkness and sprinted the shortest distance to the barrier. I reached it without meeting any resistance from the Black Organization.

"…This must be it."

I reached out and touched the thin, transparent semicircle surrounding Thousand Blade. It was at once soft and hard; it felt bizarre.

I think I can do this. I drew my sword and performed an attack with all my strength.

"Fifth Style—World Render!"

I sliced through the barrier, creating a large fissure. It spread rapidly until a piercing crack sounded, and the barrier collapsed completely.

"I did it!"

We were now able to contact the outside world. Fighting off the Black Organization wouldn't be too difficult once the holy knights or Chairwoman Reia arrived. *All we have to do now is hold out until the reinforcements arrive. The battle just turned massively in our favor!*

I sprinted to hurry back to Lia and Rose as soon as I broke the barrier. I kicked hard off the ground as I ran, and when I rounded the corner of the second school building, my breath caught in my throat.

"…How?"

I saw Lia and Rose suspended in midair by black shadows. Their limbs were restrained by tentacle-like shadows, and they were totally motionless.

"Ah-ha! What took you so long, my dearest Allen?" Dodriel said with a taunting smile as soon as he saw me. I felt my blood boil.

"…Get out of the way."

I took a step toward him and struck him with a fierce roundhouse kick to the side.

"How are you so fast?! Gaaaah!"

Dodriel went flying through the air and crashed into a school building with tremendous speed. I wasted no time freeing Lia and Rose, severing Dodriel's black shadows with one swing of my sword. I then nervously put my hands to their chests, and felt a healthy pulse from both of them.

"Thank goodness. They're okay..."

They were injured, but their wounds weren't that deep. Those shadows had probably choked them until they passed out. That was a relief.

"Ah-haaa! That's my Allen! You've gotten even stronger since the last time we met!"

I looked up and saw Dodriel getting up, brushing aside rubble from the school building. Blood ran down his face from his forehead.

"...This is the second time, Dodriel," I said. This was the second time he had hurt Lia and Rose. "I can't let this happen again... I'm gonna end you right here, right now!"

I released darkness from my entire body, enshrouding myself in a cloak of night. It was blacker than any darkness I had produced so far, and it adapted itself to my body to an unprecedented degree.

"Yes, yes! That's what I want to see, Allen! There really is no one else like you! Let's kill each other dead!"

My fated battle with Dodriel had begun.

◾

I assumed the middle stance and watched Dodriel closely. He pointed his sword at me and smiled with a complex mix of love and hate.

His Soul Attire is called Shadow Sovereign. It looked like an ordinary sword, but its ability was without equal—it made him invincible to all attacks from his opponent while he was standing in their shadow.

There has to be more to it than that, though. If that was the extent of his power, he would not have defeated Lia and Rose. I was sure he was hiding another ability up his sleeve that I had yet to see. *I should avoid close combat for now and watch his movements,* I thought.

"Allen? I'm not against standing here and losing ourselves in each other's eyes, but... aww, I hunger for more! I need your love, your blood, your life! Let the sparks fly!" Dodriel screamed nonsensically, then charged at me. "Autumn Rain Style—Rainy Season!"

He rained thrusts down upon me with no chance for rest, but it was nothing I couldn't handle. *I can see them!* I could see each thrust clearly as if time had slowed down. I dodged each one with minimal movement and performed a counterattack in sync with his blade's retreat.

"Eighth Style—Eight-Span Crow!"

"Ah-ha, that's not gonna work!"

Dodriel deflected three of the slashes and used the opening to step into my shadow. The remaining five slashes passed *through* his body.

He entered the Shadow World... Thanks to Shadow Sovereign, his body was now in another world. I could break him out using an attack as strong as World Render, but unfortunately, Dodriel was well aware of that.

"Ah-ha, I won't allow you to get me with World Render this time," he said with an innocent smile. It was as if he had read my thoughts.

"...I figured."

Dodriel had always been smart, dating back to our Grand Swordcraft Academy days. There was no way the same move would work twice against him.

"Are you ready, dear? Autumn Rain Style—Torrential Rain!"

He performed a ferocious chain of diagonal slashes, downward slashes, upward slashes, and thrusts. I could feel the malice in each swing.

"..."

I dodged some slashes, deflected others, and blocked the rest using my sword as a shield.

"Will you hold still?!" Dodriel shouted. Clearly irritated that I blocked all of his attacks, he started to swing at me even more violently. I defended myself flawlessly, feeling that something was off all the while.

Why is he resorting to such desperate chain attacks? I wasn't sure why, but that bothered me. I attended the same swordcraft academy as Dodriel for three years, so I thought I knew him better than most. *He used to pursue beauty in battle. Unleashing chain after chain is not like him. Has he just lost his temper? If so, I should take advantage,* I thought as I continued to block all of his strikes.

"Hiyaaaaa!"

Enraged, Dodriel lifted his blade high and swung it down.

This is my chance! I swung my sword up powerfully to meet his attack. "Ha!"

"What?!"

My counter caught Dodriel by surprise and pushed his arms up in the air. That left his abdomen wide open.

Now! I took a big step forward and began to perform one of my deadliest attacks. "Fifth Style—World Rend...?!" I hesitated when I saw Dodriel smile.

"Ah-ha..."

He was in what should have been dire straits, so why was he grinning? His smile conveyed intelligence, as opposed to the madness that had been evident before.

This is bad! I didn't know why, but my sixth sense was telling me that following through with the attack was a bad idea. I trusted my hunch and leaped backward—and fearsomely sharp slash attacks emerged from the shadow beneath my feet.

"Huh?!" I leaned back as far as I could to dodge the slash attacks, succeeding by a paper-thin margin.

...That was close. If I had followed through with World Render, I would've been cut in two.

"Aww, what a shame! I almost got you there! Ah-ha, ah-ha-ha, ah-ha-ha-ha-ha-ha!" Dodriel exclaimed, putting his hands on his stomach and bursting out laughing. Everything he'd done—the string of chain attacks, making it look like he'd lost his temper, and the final downward swing—had been groundwork to catch me off guard with that deadly attack.

"Oh well. My plan failed. Just the thought of your body being sliced clean in two... Oh, I can't help but smile!" he sang, hugging himself and squirming.

I ignored his eccentric provocation and asked a question. "Did you just *teleport* that slash attack?"

The location he swung his sword and the location the slash attack occurred were not the same. In other words, he'd sent his move to a *different space.*

"Very good, Allen! That's exactly right! My Shadow Sovereign is capable of ranged slash attacks!"

"Ranged slash attacks?"

"Yes! I can transport a slash attack from my shadow into any adjoining shadow... Just like this!"

Dodriel swung his sword, and a sharp slash attack flew out of my shadow. "Nrgh..." I erased the slice with a horizontal sweep of my blade.

"Useful, right? And look at that perfectly cloudy sky! Clouds cast shadows, meaning this entire area is under my domain! Ah-ha, it's as if God himself is on my side!" he shouted, throwing his arms wide and beaming.

"...You've done a great job drawing out your Soul Attire's power," I said. He wasn't called a prodigy for nothing; he may have lost his mind, but his talent was as elite as ever.

"Thanks, but your praise brings me no joy... By the way, did you know that Soul Attire becomes stronger the more you walk the line between life and... *death!*" Dodriel said, thrusting his sword toward me in sync with the last word.

"The line between life and death... Do you mean almost dying?" I asked as I defended myself.

"Exactly! When serious wounds threaten to snuff out your life, you experience the interval between life and death—between the material and the immaterial! That ties the body and soul closer together, causing your Soul Attire to shine ever brighter!"

"Huh, I didn't know that."

I had a sense for what he was talking about. I'd emerged from my duels against Shido and Idora inexplicably stronger despite being gravely injured in both fights. *I thought I had just gained confidence and skill from the experience of defeating strong opponents, but...* It seemed like there was a theory to explain the phenomenon I'd experienced.

"While you've been sitting fat and happy at Thousand Blade Academy, I've spent day after day fighting my way through countless battlefields. I've groveled through mud, I've struggled to find food, I've killed people... All to get revenge on you for ruining my life!" he bellowed, his face twisted with hate.

...He's broken. Dodriel's personality had been shattered beyond repair. The trigger was probably our duel from one year ago. He'd lost to me in front of a large crowd that he gathered, despite having spent

the last three years ridiculing me as the Reject Swordsman. That had wounded his delicate pride.

He has every right to resent me for that, but... This was a seed that I had planted. I was going to settle the matter once and for all.

"You've been leading an easy life at your cozy swordcraft academy... Do you really think you can defeat me?! Autumn Rain Secret Technique—Downpour!" Dodriel yelled wide-eyed, performing a thrust with all his strength behind it.

"I know I can," I replied casually, swinging down my mock black sword hardened by darkness.

"Graaaah!"

My attack tore through the Shadow World and carved a deep slash wound into his chest.

"N-noooooooooo! M-my precious world!"

Dodriel seemed more distraught by how I destroyed his Shadow World in one swing than he was by the gash in his chest.

"It's evident in your blade that you really have struggled through much strife and bloodshed. But I have spent every day working tirelessly at my swordcraft as well," I said.

Lia, Rose, Shido, Idora—I hadn't faced a single easy opponent. It had felt like my life was on the line with every fight. My days at Thousand Blade had been anything but easy.

I watched Dodriel intently, and he glared back at me with bloodshot eyes.

"I'm *sick* of your goddamn face, Reject Swordsman! Just how long are you going to be a thorn in my side?!" he screamed furiously, coiling dreadful black shadow around his sword. It was corrupt and repulsive, an extraordinary conglomeration of negative power. He was likely planning on ending our duel with one all-out attack.

"Let's do this, Allen!"

"Bring it on!"

Dodriel swung his sword as our shouts echoed around us.

"Die—Shadow Phantom!"

He sent a torrent of shadow waves rushing at me with astounding speed. The overpowering, violent mass engulfed the surrounding trees and rubble.

I lifted my sword above my head and swung it down resolutely.

"Sixth Style—Dark Boom!"

I sent an enormous slash attack coated in darkness toward Dodriel, and it gouged the earth as it raced toward him. An instant later, the pitch-black darkness and the hollow shadow collided violently. The collision produced an incredible shock wave, which inflicted a large crack in the main school building. Our attacks appeared to be an equal match at first, but the all-destroying black Dark Boom broke through and engulfed Dodriel. His pitiful scream echoed across the campus.

"N-no... THAT'S IMPOSSIBLE!!!!!"

"Did I do it?" I waited for the smoke to clear, and then saw him gasping on two legs. "...He's really tough," I said to myself right as he collapsed to the ground face-first.

"Haah, haah... Damn, it...," he muttered. He had deep gashes all over his body; I doubted he could fight any longer.

"This is it. The holy knights will be here shortly. Stay put until then," I ordered before turning my back on him.

"Ah-ha-ha... You're such a... nice person, Allen... To think you'd feel pity for...a piece of trash like me... You're so naive it makes me want to vomit!" Dodriel yelled, and an eerie shadow wrapped around his entire body.

"Huh?!" I leaped back hurriedly and assumed the middle stance.

"Hmm-hmm-hmm, ah-ha-ha, ah-ha-ha-ha-ha-ha-ha!"

He laughed cacophonously as the black shadow adhered to his body like some kind of tattoo. *His wounds are closing.* The substance pulled his wounds shut and stopped the bleeding.

"Ah-ha... I feel so strong I could tear even the Thirteen Oracle Knights limb from limb!" Dodriel proclaimed.

He swung his sword at the main school building as if testing himself, and blasted away a wall, revealing the classroom inside. *He did that with one swing?! How did he get so strong?!* That shadow must have greatly enhanced his physical strength.

"Shadow and darkness... What are the odds we'd both end up with different shades of black?! It's fitting for a fallen prodigy and the Reject Swordsman, don't you think?"

I ignored Dodriel's nonsense and studied his body closely.

"That power... You're pushing yourself too hard," I said.

I could see that the shadow was pressing so tightly against his body that he'd started to bleed all over. It looked like he was straining his very cells to function beyond their natural limit.

"No, I'm not! This pain is good for me! Enduring agony is how you become stronger! All right, Allen...let's grow and reach for new heights together!" Dodriel yelled with a wicked grin, taking an aggressive forward-bent posture.

"Sorry, but your growth ends right here, right now," I said.

I covered my body with a denser darkness than ever before, and assumed the middle stance. Our eyes crossed, enveloped in darkness and shadow, black against black.

"Let's do this, Dodriel!"

"Ah-ha, show me what you've got, Allen!"

I gripped the mock-black sword tightly and entered range with one step.

"Eighth Style—Eight-Span Crow!"

I performed an eight-part slash attack aimed accurately for his vital points.

"Predictable! Autumn Rain Style—Misty Rain!"

Dodriel met my technique with an inverted slash. Eight-Span Crow and Misty Rain collided and canceled each other out.

What?! I covered that slash with darkness! Dodriel's strength, sword speed, and reaction time had all increased significantly.

"Come on, Allen... What the hell are you so surprised about?!" he yelled, seeing my discomposure. He kicked at me powerfully and precisely, and I whipped my sword horizontally to block it. "Ngh?!" Despite my perfect defense, it felt like both of my palms had been bludgeoned with a club.

Holy cow... He surpasses Shido in terms of pure strength... His kick sent me flying backward, but I kept my head up so Dodriel wouldn't leave my sight.

"I'm not close to being done!" Dodriel shouted.

"Grk, come at me!" I challenged.

Dodriel attacked ferociously, and I did my best to ward him off. That exchange continued for quite some time.

"YAAAAAAAAAAA!"

He swung his sword like a hurricane, his attacks coming without pause.

"…"

His assault was fierce and relentless. I kept my eyes wide open and focused all of my mental energy into defending myself, but my injuries built up over time.

Dammit... I've managed to avoid a lethal wound, but my disadvantage is only growing..., I thought, gritting my teeth.

"Blaargh."

Dodriel then suddenly vomited blood. He leaped back in retreat and wiped his mouth with a sleeve.

"Ah-ha... Looks like I'm...reaching my limit...," he said.

Dark-red blood was oozing from Dodriel's every pore. The shadow was automatically forcing the wounds shut to try to stop the bleeding, but he was past his physical limit, and his body was breaking down too quickly for his recovery rate to handle. Binding with the shadow to enable superhuman movement must have placed an enormous burden on himself.

I've won. I still had plenty of darkness left, and it was only a matter of time before Dodriel self-destructed. *I need to carry Lia and Rose to safety once this is over. I'll join the president on the front line after that.*

"I wish this could last forever, but let's move on to the final act!" Dodriel yelled, throwing his arms wide. A giant mass of shadow then formed in the air behind him. Its surface rippled unevenly, and it looked at once like a cocoon and a ball of black water.

What is that...? I maintained the middle stance and directed my attention to the strange mass.

"Ah-ha-ha, don't you look away from me!"

Suddenly, Dodriel was right in my face.

"Take this!" he yelled, swinging his sword down savagely from above his head. I just barely blocked it, but he wasn't done yet. "Dark Shadow!"

I felt a stabbing sense of malice from behind me. *This is bad...* I knew without even turning around that the mass of shadow that had been behind Dodriel was now behind me.

"*Hraagh!*" I acted quickly and formed a *wall of darkness* behind me, just in time to stop ten tentacles millimeters before me. They had shot out of the mass of shadow. The tentacles might have been strong, but they weren't powerful enough to pierce through the darkness.

That was close. If my decision had come even a fraction of a second later, I would have been punched full of holes.

I jumped to the side to distance myself from Dodriel and his mass of shadow.

"Ah-ha... Well done blocking that! You really are special, Allen! Those pathetic girls didn't stand a chance in hell against it!" Dodriel said, mocking Lia and Rose.

So that's the attack that knocked them out... It was impossible to be prepared for that pincer attack without knowing it was coming. I would've been in big trouble if I didn't have the darkness.

Man, this ability is a real handful... It seemed like Dark Shadow— the black mass—could teleport just like the ranged slashes.

"Ahhh, I love that pale look on your face... Seeing it makes me want to tear your body into a thousand tiny little pieces!" he screamed fanatically, and rushed toward me. "Dance with me, Allen Rodol!"

"..."

He forced me into a lengthy defensive struggle.

"What are you waiting for, Allen?! You'll never beat me if you keep running!"

"Ngh..."

Dodriel pressed me at close range while skillfully controlling the ten tentacles, and my injuries steadily piled up. *He's ridiculous...* The fight was one blade versus eleven— his sword plus the ten tentacles. I was at a huge numbers disadvantage.

...Should I do it? If I enveloped my body with all the darkness I had,

I could probably neutralize Dark Shadow. That would eliminate the tentacles and put us on equal footing. All I would have to do then was wait for Dodriel's body to break down.

What about after the fight, though? Could I defend Lia and Rose if I used that significant an amount of spirit power? Could I help Shii and the others fighting on the front line?

"Hey, Allen... You're not thinking about what you're going to do after our duel, are you?" Dodriel asked.

"...You saw right through me," I admitted. It seemed like he could read my thoughts as well as I could read his.

"Duels between swordsmen are fights to the death! You shouldn't think about anything other than stopping your opponent's heart!" he yelled, and resumed his torrent of attacks.

"Hrk..." One of the tentacles sliced me on the shoulder, sending blood flying through the air. Meanwhile, Dodriel continued to bleed as his shadow ripped up his skin.

"Hey, come on! Keep your eyes on me... Don't think about anyone but *me!*" he said, practically in tears, swinging his sword again and again. I thought about what he said as I defended myself.

He's right, I was thinking about what I was going to do next. I'd allowed my mind to wander during a life-or-death duel with Dodriel. That was an insult to your opponent. *He's literally putting his life on the line in this fight...* As a swordsman, I needed to match his effort with everything I had.

"Sorry about that, Dodriel. You're right—duels between swordsmen are serious business," I apologized. "I won't let my mind wander again. I'm going to give this fight my all!"

I unleashed every last bit of darkness I had. It painted the area around us black, creating an ebon stage for us to fight on. It was even denser than when I'd fought Idora, and so dark it looked like an abyss.

"That's spectacular, Allen! You always far exceed my expectations! That was true even then, you know! I both love and hate you for it!" he screamed with satisfaction, his face lit by ecstasy.

"HAAAAAAAAAAA!!"

"OOOOOOOOOH!!"

Then as if we had arranged it beforehand, we charged at each other simultaneously.

"Cherry Blossom Blade Secret Technique—Mirror Sakura Slash!"

"Autumn Rain Secret Technique—Downpour!"

Our slash attacks collided violently, sending sparks flying before both vanished. We wasted no time, simultaneously performing downward diagonal slices that resulted in the screech of metal on metal. Our swords locked, and our eyes met.

"You really are strong...Dodriel...!"

"What, did you just notice? Know your place, Reject Swordsman!"

We both put all our weight and strength behind our swords as we struggled for dominance.

"*Hrragh!*" I yelled.

"D-dammit...," he cursed.

Masked in darkness, I won our contest of strength and sent him flying. I had set a trap in the direction that I sent him.

"Second Style—Hazy Moon!"

"What the?!"

The slash attack I had set during our duel sliced his thighs.

"...Goddammit," he cursed.

I sprinted forward to attack Dodriel while he was vulnerable on the ground.

"Eighth Style—Eight-Span Crow!"

"Not so fast! Dark Shadow!"

He countered with absolute perfect timing, but it still wasn't good enough.

"Ha!"

I released darkness from my entire body and engulfed the incoming shadow.

"Wh-what?!"

The eight slashes struck him in his moment of discomposure.

"Gaaa!"

Dodriel was heavily injured. He leaped backward in retreat and used the shadow to force his wounds shut. Our deadly bout seemed to go on forever.

"Haah, haah…"

"Ah-ha, ah-ha-ha… Your strength is truly impressive, Allen…"

It wouldn't be long before we both ran out of spirit power. *He would be no match for me in a standard sword fight.* Despite that, Dodriel would not be defeated. No matter how many times I broke skin, no matter how many times I nearly inflicted a fatal wound, he lifted his head and fought to hang on. His will to win was overriding his physical limits.

"Haah, haah… Let's end this!" I shouted.

"Ah-ha… I don't want to, but it looks like we have no choice…," he responded.

The darkness enshrouding my body was weakening, and the shadow covering his body was thinning. We were both near our limit. Our next technique would likely be our last. Resolving myself, I sheathed my sword.

"It's time, Dodriel!"

"Show me what you've got, Allen!"

We shared a brief exchange, and I rushed at him barehanded. *My darkness is too weak right now to block his Dark Shadow.* His weapons still greatly outnumbered mine. That meant I needed to render that disadvantage meaningless by using my fastest attack!

"Diiiieee! Autumn Rain Secret Technique—Downpour! Dark Shadow!"

He thrust his sword at me along with twenty tentacles at tremendous speed. I could feel the malice and hatred behind his attack. I studied the approaching assault and readied my fastest attack.

"Seventh Style—Draw Flash!" I yelled, performing a draw strike that surpassed the speed of sound.

"Gah…"

It tore through Dark Shadow and struck Dodriel. I turned around just in time to see him slowly collapse to the ground.

"Phew… That was close." I let out a sigh of relief at having won my deadly duel with Dodriel—and then an ear-splitting boom reverberated throughout Thousand Blade.

"Wh-what was that sound?!"

It came from the schoolyard where Shii and the others were fighting.

I have a bad feeling about this. Whatever it was would have to wait—the first priority was carrying Lia and Rose to safety. *I'll take them to the staff room for now.*

Having defeated my longtime rival Dodriel, I picked up the unconscious pair of girls and headed for the staff room.

■

I ran down the long hallways and passed through the open door of the staff room. The deputy chairman noticed me right away.

"H-hey, it's Allen! Thank goodness you're safe… Wh-what happened to Lia and Rose?!" he asked wide-eyed when he saw their limp bodies.

"Don't worry, they're just unconscious," I told him.

"That's a relief… I'm surprised to see you so heavily injured. You must have encountered a formidable opponent."

"Yes, and I only barely won. By the way, have you reached out for help yet from outside the academy? I destroyed the barrier."

He grinned in response to my question.

"That is all taken care of! The chairwoman should arrive in about five minutes. Of course, we contacted the Holy Knights Association, too. You did great, Allen!"

"That's good."

Victory would be as good as ours as soon as Chairwoman Reia arrived. *We're almost out of the woods!* I was going to do what I could in the meantime.

"All right, I'm going to go join the president and the others," I said, and started to leave the staff room.

"Wait, Allen. You can't. You have to run," the deputy chairman responded, grabbing my shoulder. He had a serious look in his eyes.

"Wh-why?" I stammered.

"We received a message from one of the teachers on the front line… A member of the Thirteen Oracle Knights has been spotted among the enemy forces. Not even you would stand a chance in your injured state," he explained.

"…The Thirteen Oracle Knights?" I repeated. I was pretty sure Dodriel had mentioned them during our duel.

"They are the senior management of the Black Organization. Every one of them is an elite swordfighter with strength to match an entire country's military. They are said to be as strong as the Elite Five Academy chairs."

"Th-they're as strong as Chairwoman Reia?!"

"That's right. Challenging one of the Thirteen Oracle Knights is equivalent to taking on an entire country. So please, Allen. Get out of here while you can."

"If what you say is true, I need to give my support."

I couldn't run away after hearing that. I wouldn't be able to bear the shame.

"Huh?! Why do you say that?!"

"The president and everyone else are fighting to protect the academy from an enemy of that caliber as we speak. I can't turn tail and run just to save myself."

There was only so much I could do with my minimal strength. But in battle, the difference in size between opposing forces was very important. Even adding one person to the defense would help.

"Thank you for your concern," I said, and left the staff room.

"Hey, wait! Allen! Dammit... Please, Chairwoman, get here as fast as you can..."

■

I ignored the deputy chairman's attempts to stop me and headed for the schoolyard. I couldn't believe my eyes when I arrived.

"What happened here...?"

The schoolyard had been turned into a desolate wasteland, and my fellow Thousand Blade students were collapsed throughout it. A tall, slender man was standing calmly among them.

That bastard... I felt rage boil up, but shook my head to calm myself. I then walked toward Shii, who was lying facedown on the ground, while being careful to keep the man in my sight.

"President, are you okay?" I asked, gently shaking her shoulders.

"A-Allen...? G-get away from here... That monster...can't be beat...," she muttered before losing consciousness.

So he's that strong. Shii was the biggest sore loser I knew; if she said he was unbeatable, he must be a truly elite swordsman. He was too much for me in my wounded state.

But I don't have a choice. I was the only swordsman left at Thousand Blade who could still fight. If I ran, there was a chance everyone here would be killed. *Also, Chairwoman Reia will be here at any moment. I just need to buy time until then.*

My mind made up, I raised my guard to its highest level and approached the person responsible for all this destruction.

"...Are you the one who did this?" I demanded.

"Hmm? Yes, I am. I grew tired of these insects and their buzzing, so I simply swatted them away," he answered coolly.

"...Did you just call them 'insects'?"

Hearing him insult my friends brought the anger I had just repressed back to the surface.

"You're Allen Rodol, correct?"

"...?!"

He somehow knew my name.

"No need to look so surprised. I've only seen your name in reports. They mentioned a child with some small amount of skill."

"...I don't like you knowing my name without me knowing yours. Want to introduce yourself?" I asked. I wanted to keep him talking to buy time.

"Hmm, you have a point. I am Fuu Ludoras, one of the Thirteen Oracle Knights. A pleasure to make your acquaintance," he said politely with a slight bow. He seemed like a talkative type.

Fuu Ludoras stood at over 190 centimeters tall. His long black hair reached his back. He was thin for a swordsman and likely in his early thirties. His chiseled and handsome face gave him an intellectual impression; without his sword, he would have looked like a scholar.

He wore a red noble's jacket, and a black cloak emblazoned with a giant green pattern I felt like I had seen somewhere before. The cloak looked different from the overcoats the rank-and-file members of the Black Organization wore; it probably signified high status.

"Are you all after Lia?" I inquired.

"...Lia? Ah, that is the name of Fafnir's current host, isn't it...," he responded, putting his hand to his chin as if trying to jog his memory.

"Fafnir's...host?"

"Just so. We are gathering eidolons, starting with the Primal Dragon King. Strictly speaking, the girl means nothing to us. We need what's inside her."

"There's an...eidolon inside her?"

Shii mentioned that word at lunch earlier.

"Hmm... I don't mind a good chat, and I especially enjoy seeing youth full of intellectual curiosity. I'd like to sit down for some tea, but unfortunately, I don't have the time. That will have to wait for another opportunity."

Fuu readied a thin sword that looked like a rapier.

"Huh?!"

When he did so, he began to radiate a thick, suffocating malice.

"What's wrong, Allen Rodol? Don't you know how to fight?" Fuu asked, and I realized I was standing there defenseless.

"Grr... HAAAAAAAA!"

I scrounged together what little spirit power I had left and covered myself in thick darkness. I had rested enough to regain a little spirit power. *I feel like I can last a few minutes!*

I assumed the middle stance...

"What are you looking at?"

"Huh?!"

...And suddenly, Fuu was right behind me.

"Hya!"

"Nnn..."

He swung mercilessly for my neck. I instantly kicked off the ground and dodged by a paper-thin margin.

"Impressive reaction speed," he said.

Fuu went for the kill without any hesitation. His greater level of experience could not have been more evident.

He'll kill me if I get stuck on the defensive... Offense was the best defense. I dropped my center of gravity, and closed the distance between us as quickly as I could.

"Eighth Style—Eight-Span Crow!"

"Wind Barrier."

I performed Eight-Span Crow with all my might, but he blocked it easily using an invisible barrier.

"What?!"

"Never show discomposure during combat. Severing Gale."

He fired a powerful gust of wind that hit me square in the stomach. "Gah?!" It was so painful it felt like my stomach had been carved open. The force blasted me backward, and I tumbled on the ground unable to regain my balance.

"...Hmm, it appears you have already spent a considerable amount of energy. But you move impressively considering your lack of Soul Attire... It would be a shame to kill such an outstanding talent," he muttered leisurely.

This is bad... I can't beat him... He was said to have the strength of a nation's entire military. I hadn't even realized my Soul Attire yet; as much as it pained me to admit, I wasn't ready to fight someone like him yet. *That may be true, but retreat isn't an option!* I needed to do my best to hold on for the few minutes it would take for Chairwoman Reia to arrive!

My body was screaming with pain, but I forced myself to stand anyway.

"So you can still stand. Your physical strength and mental fortitude are impressive," Fuu said.

"Haah, haah... I-I'm not done!" I yelled. I poured all the darkness I had left into a true last-ditch attack. "Sixth Style—Dark Boom!"

An enormous slash attack coated in pitch-black darkness rushed toward Fuu.

"Supreme Wind Blade!"

Unfortunately, he summoned a large blade of wind and easily tore through the black Dark Boom.

"Wh-what the?!"

The black Dark Boom had never once been torn apart like that. *How did he destroy it so easily...?* I stood dumbfounded at the hopeless sight. A second later, the still immensely strong Supreme Wind Blade stabbed me.

"Ga-hah..."

The wound inflicted by the wind blade was deep. Too deep. There was no way I would be able to continue fighting.

Dammit... I fell to my hands and knees, clenching my teeth hard. Fuu then looked up and said something I couldn't believe.

"Hmm. He gave you quite the beating, Dodriel."

"Ah-ha, sorry about that, boss... But I've secured Fafnir!"

Dodriel jumped down from the second story of the school building. He was covered in blood. A black shadow floated behind him, and Lia was suspended within it.

"L-Lia?!" I said in shock. I had just taken her to the staff room.

"How's it going, Allen?" Dodriel taunted, leaning his face directly into mine. He had somehow fully recovered.

"H-how did you...?!"

I had undoubtedly hit him with Draw Flash. There was no way he should have been back on his feet like this.

"Ha-ha-ha, you wouldn't believe the scientific advancements we've made... Just look at this incredible recovery medicine!" he said, pulling a blue pill out of his pocket.

"Is that a soul-crystal pill?!" I exclaimed.

I looked closely and saw a large distortion in Dodriel's Shadow Sovereign.

"Correctamundo! This is the heavily improved second generation of soul-crystal pills. In exchange for just a small fraction of your life span, you can instantly recover from anything!" Dodriel explained.

"Dodriel, don't be so ready to volunteer company secrets," Fuu reprimanded.

"Ah-ha, sorry...," Dodriel apologized.

I calmly steadied my breathing as they talked. *I think three minutes have passed since I started buying time.* That meant I just needed to last two more minutes. In two more minutes, Chairwoman Reia would get here. *I have to last, no matter what it takes...*

I squeezed out what little strength I had left in my legs and stood up slowly. "...Huh?" I then felt a peculiar pain in my chest that I had never experienced before.

"Ah-ha, duels between swordsmen are fights to the death! That means I win, Allen."

Dodriel's face was twisted with joy. I looked down and saw that his blade had plunged deep into my chest.

No...

I felt pain. Hot, searing agony.

I can't...breathe... A metallic taste filled my mouth as burning pain raced through my body. I leaned against Dodriel and then fell forward limply to the ground.

"Ah-ha, ah-ha-ha-ha-ha... Ah-ha-ha-ha-ha-ha-ha-ha!"

His maniacal laugh assaulted my ears. As my vision began to blur, I saw Lia restrained by shadow. "Li...a..." I mustered the last of my strength to reach out my hand, but grabbed only air.

My consciousness faded to black.

■

Dodriel had just stabbed Allen in the heart.

"Th-that felt so good...!" he said, smiling with a complex mixture of pleasure, excitement, and sorrow. "Ha-ha... Ah-ha-ha, ah-ha-ha-ha, ahhhh-ha-ha-ha-ha-ha-ha!"

His laughter sounded like the hollow wailing of a man who had accomplished his life's goal of revenge.

"...That was a bit of a waste," Fuu muttered, then turned to Dodriel. "We've obtained Fafnir. It's time to get out of here. We have intel that Black Fist is headed here now, and the Blood Fox resides in this country as well. Let's not dawdle."

"Ah-ha, yes, sir..."

They turned around to leave, and then suddenly a deep darkness enshrouded the entire Thousand Blade campus.

""What?!""

The darkness extended as far as the eye could see. Fuu and Dodriel both drew their swords in response to this unprecedented situation.

Don't tell me... An absurd possibility occurred to Fuu. There was only one swordsman present who could wield darkness: Allen Rodol, who Dodriel had just slain. *But he was stabbed through the heart! I saw him die!*

Fuu turned around slowly.

"Pfft, gwa-ha-ha-ha-ha! Man, the air outside tastes so sweet..."

There stood Allen Rodol, uninjured and cackling heartily. His hair had grown long and turned bone white. A black pattern had formed under his left eye, which had turned a brilliant shade of crimson along with his right. But his looks weren't the only thing that had transformed—nothing about the ferocious expression lining his face resembled Allen in the slightest. It was as if he had morphed into a different person entirely. Fuu and Dodriel were in shock.

"You have my thanks, worms... You dumbasses gave me the chance to come to the surface!" Allen proclaimed. Cloaked in darkness on an entirely different level of quality and volume, he casually produced an ebon blade.

""...?!""

As soon as he did so, Fuu and Dodriel were assaulted by a pressure so great it felt as if their bodies were being crushed. They gasped simultaneously, immediately grasping how much power their opponent was now emanating.

"...Dodriel, give me your support."

"...Yes, sir."

And thus, a new fight to the death had begun.

◾

Allen Rodol versus Fuu and Dodriel. In a battle that was equivalent to a clash of nations, Fuu made the first move.

"Severing Gale Seal!"

He swung his rapier down, causing compressed gusts of wind to assail Allen from four sides, each one tremendously fast. This technique would have instantly killed an ordinary sword wielder.

This is my fastest attack! What's going to happen?! Fuu waited for Allen's response and prepared himself vigilantly for a follow-up strike.

"What the...?!" Allen said. For some reason, he didn't move as he watched the slash attacks rush toward him. The four fearsomely powerful gusts of wind hit him head-on less than a second later, resulting in a deafening boom and a huge cloud of dust.

"...Did I hit him?" Fuu said aloud, staggering a step backward with surprise at the unexpected outcome of his attack. "Th-that's impossible!"

The dust cleared to reveal an uninjured Allen, a vicious smile on his face.

"Pfft, gwa-ha-ha-ha-ha! What, was that gentle breeze supposed to hurt me?! First ice and now wind..." Allen burst out laughing, remembering his duel with Shido. "You guys are somethin' else! ...Are you mocking me?!"

His mood swung wildly from jovial laughter to seething rage. *Here he comes...* Fuu devoted his full attention to carefully observing Allen's every move. "...Huh?" But before he knew it, Allen was right in his face with his left fist raised.

"*Hrrraaaagh!*" Allen screamed, swinging his fist forward in a brutally violent left straight punch.

"W-Wind Barrier!" Fuu immediately produced an invisible shield made of compressed wind. The wind was outward-facing and powerful, and provided infallible protection from physical attacks. At least, that should have been the case.

"The hell is this flimsy shield...? Take this seriously!" Allen yelled. He easily smashed the wind barrier to pieces with his fist and struck Fuu deep in the abdomen.

"Oooof!"

The dull sound of bones breaking reverberated upon contact, and Fuu was sent flying backward high into the air.

"Ha-ha, look at him go!" Allen laughed, watching leisurely as Fuu soared through the sky. You would have had no idea he was in the middle of combat.

"Die—Dark Shadow!"

Dodriel took advantage by sending twenty tentacles at Allen, a shadow chain attack strong enough to punch through iron. Every single one struck Allen.

"…Did I get him?" Just as his lips began to curl into a smile, he heard laughing from behind him.

"Pfft, you talkin' about me?"

"Huh?!" Dodriel turned around in a panic and received a fierce roundhouse kick to his side. "Grrgh?!" It was the most painful blow he had ever experienced, and he was sent bouncing on the ground, unable to regain his balance.

"Huh? Good lord, is the fight over already?" Allen said in disbelief.

Fuu Ludoras was one of the Thirteen Oracle Knights, each of whom were supposed to have the strength to match an entire nation. Dodriel Barton was considered a leading candidate to become their next member. And yet, Allen had finished each of them off in a single blow. He sighed in disappointment.

"All right… Who's next?" he said, eyeing the remaining members of the Black Organization who had been watching the beatdown in dumbfounded silence. It was like he was searching for his next toy.

"""" """"
……

Some collapsed where they stood, some wept silently, and others foamed at the mouth and fainted. The terror was too much for them to handle.

"Gwa-ha-ha-ha-ha! It's been ages since I've been in the outside world. There'll be no harm in helping me with a little rehab," Allen said. To him, this violent display was nothing more than getting back into shape.

A savage gust of wind whooshed toward him. "…Huh?" He easily avoided the clearly man-made wind, and looked toward its source.

"This isn't over, you monster."

"Allen…I will never allow myself to lose to you…"

Fuu and Dodriel were standing there, both fully recovered. They were holding unstable Soul Attire.

"What, you can still stand? Maybe you guys can amuse me for a bit after all!" Allen said with a wicked smile, slightly raising his estimation of the toys before him. At first he thought they were junk that would break instantly upon contact; now they were at least junk that could take a small beating.

Meanwhile, Fuu and Dodriel conferred in a whisper.

"That was your second one, right? Can you still fight, Dodriel?"

"Ah-ha... Honestly, it's all I can do just to stand..."

They had both clung to life after receiving their lethal wounds by immediately taking a soul-crystal pill. They were the second generation of soul-crystal pills, given only to top management and those close to them. Thanks to many experiments, the side effects had been greatly suppressed and the self-recovery ability enhanced. However, it was unsafe to take more than one a day. Any more than that would invite pain so immense that even standing would take a herculean effort.

"...It would be best if we could flee immediately, but I'm afraid that demon won't let us get away," said Fuu.

"...You've got that right," Dodriel agreed.

After preparing himself mentally for further combat, Fuu began to give Dodriel instructions.

"We have no chance in close combat given his preposterous physical strength. Let's muster all our spirit power and bury him with our strongest long-distance attacks!"

"Yes, sir!"

They wasted no time.

"Severing Gale Seal!"

"Shadow Phantom!"

They summoned all their strength and sent a blitzing stream of wind blades sharp enough to cut through anything and an all-engulfing stream of shadow. It was an attack devastating enough to turn the entirety of Thousand Blade into a wasteland.

Allen tilted his head as if in thought. "Hrmm... What does that brat call it again?" he said. "Oh, that's it. Let's see... First Style—Flying Shadow!" He swung his sword down, creating a destructive wave of pitch-black darkness that annihilated Fuu's and Dodriel's all-out attacks.

"H-his strength is...unfathomable...," gasped Fuu.

"...Ha-ha, we're doomed," laughed Dodriel in resignation.

The darkness swallowed them both in an instant, and silence fell upon Thousand Blade Academy.

"Gwa-ha-ha-ha-ha-ha-ha-ha! Come on, that was just a light swing! Don't tell me that was enough to kill them!" Allen yelled, bursting out laughing.

Fuu landed behind him, covered in blood. He had avoided the darkness by enveloping his body in wind and flying into the air at the last possible moment.

"You're dead—Supreme Wind Blade!" He performed his ultimate move with all of his remaining spirit power behind it. The distance, the timing, and the aim could not have been more perfect. The attack had one purpose—to kill Allen. Even then, however, his blade failed to penetrate the cloak of darkness that Allen had casually coated himself with.

"Ha… It's hard as steel." His will to fight broken, all Fuu could do was laugh.

"Good lord, do you think this is a game? I even gave you a chance there, and you went and wasted it."

Allen casually kicked Fuu in the chest, crushing his ribs. Fuu was sent flying, and he finally came to fully grasp the difference in strength between them. *Ha-ha, what is this monster and where did he come from...?*

There was nothing Fuu could do to win. Allen's overwhelming strength made that abundantly clear. Knowing that, he took his second soul-crystal pill of the day.

"…"

Searing pain raced through him as if all his blood vessels were going to explode. *You're not supposed to take two for a reason...* Fuu did his best to bear the overwhelming pain and raised his voice for all his subordinates to hear.

"Retreat! I hereby declare Allen Rodol an S-class threat! He is more dangerous than an eidolon! Everyone, your top priority is now escaping with your life and delivering this information to headquarters!" he ordered.

"""Yes, sir!""" They all replied, just a moment before the black sword flew into their midst.

"Huh?!" Fuu shouted.

With a boom that was loud enough to be heard all throughout Aurest, the hundred-plus remaining Black Organization members were all killed. Fuu stared dumbfounded at the bottomless hole that had been opened in the schoolyard. Allen had caused that destruction with but one throw of his black sword.

"Who're you talkin' to, you creep? There's no one here but us," Allen taunted with a mean smile. He was suddenly holding a second black sword.

"Allen Rodol... Ha-ha, if I had known a monster like you would be here, I would not have accepted this jo—Gaaah!"

Fuu had thrown down his blade and admitted defeat, but Allen punched him square in the face. A gruesome sound echoed through the schoolyard, and he lost consciousness.

After easily knocking out two swordsmen with the strength to rival nations, Allen felt a strong sense of dissatisfaction.

"Haahhh... That didn't even make for a good warmup," he said, clicking his tongue and stretching. Chairwoman Reia Lasnote then appeared before him. She had been waiting for the right moment to strike after arriving a minute earlier, knowing that the arrogant and overconfident "Allen Rodol" would eventually let his guard down.

"Swordless Style—Sever!"

Reia punched her fist forward in a carefully aimed thrust, but caught only air. *How did he dodge my fist from this close?! My timing was perfect!* Her face flushed red after letting her best chance slip away.

"Hey, Black Fist. How's it goin'?"

Reia then heard a despair-inducing voice from behind her. Spirit Cores had one weakness that could be used to defeat them without fail: initial petrification. Now that that had passed, she had no chance of victory.

"Horrible, thanks to you. I see you emerged from that world?" Reia responded.

"Ha-ha, it kinda just happened. I got lucky... Hragh!" Allen yelled, perfectly copying the thrust that he just saw Reia perform.

"Blargh!"

Allen's thrust surpassed the speed of sound and pulverized Reia's ribs. He then casually kicked her and pivoted on his heel.

"N-no, wait!" Reia called after him.

"I don't have time to waste talkin' to you. He's gonna wake up soon... If you're worried about the brat, don't be. I'll give him this body back before long," Allen said.

◼

Deep in the mountains in the middle of nowhere, an old man was fishing and humming cheerfully.

"Hyo-hoh-hoh, that's a big one! I'm gonna have a feast tonight!"

Allen then landed before him, looking relaxed from his light exercise.

"Hey, you old fart. You really half-assed this, didn't you?"

"Hyo-hoh... D-don't be so mad at me... I-I didn't have any idea Allen Rodol was going to be this great of a swordsman...!" the old man pleaded.

"Ha, I don't give a crap about that. Anyway, there's no time—let's begin."

"Hyo-hoh-hoh, understood."

Allen Rodol and the Time Hermit began a strategy meeting that transcended time.

◼

I awoke to warm sunlight.

"...Hmm?"

I became aware of my surroundings as my consciousness came into focus. I smelled fresh blades of grass, I heard the chirping of birds, and felt a pleasant breeze on my skin.

"Where am I...?"

I sat up and looked around to see that I was surrounded by lush trees. I had been sleeping in a forest.

"H-huh...? Why was I sleeping here?"

My body was light as a feather, but my head felt like a bag of bricks. *Oh yeah... The Thousand Blade Festival was yesterday. I went through the haunted house with Lia and Rose...then I played poker with the president during the shadow festival...then Tessa got a little carried away at the celebration party...then... Huh?* I couldn't remember anything after that.

"...It's not coming to me. Guess I'll try walking around."

I was surely just groggy. Deciding that was all it was, I started walking through the forest. I realized where I was after about two or three minutes. *It's been a long time.* This was a small forest near Ms. Paula's dorm. I trained here often when I attended Grand Swordcraft Academy, so I knew the landscape well.

"This means *that* should be around here somewhere..." I searched around, relying on my memory—and there it was. "Ha-ha, this is kind of nostalgic."

I picked up the 100-Million-Year Button that I had tossed onto the ground and abandoned here. It glowed with an alluring red light. This was where everything started.

"What in the world *was* that place...?"

Reflecting absentmindedly on that strange experience, I pushed the button. Nothing happened. That wasn't surprising; it was broken, after all. I looked closely and saw that a large gash had been carved into the back. That must have been from when I'd broken out of the Prison of Time.

"I wonder what the Time Hermit is up to now...?"

According to Chairwoman Reia, he was wandering the world, handing the 100-Million-Year Button to people with talent. His motive was unclear, but he must have been working toward some sort of objective.

"Well, I'll probably never see him again," I said, returning the 100-Million-Year Button to where I'd found it. "I might as well go pay Ms. Paula a visit now that I'm here."

I walked toward her dorm to see her for the first time in half a year.

■

Heading through the forest that had become a backyard of sorts during my time at Grand Swordcraft Academy, I arrived at Ms. Paula's dorm.

"Something smells good."

An alluring scent drifted outdoors and whetted my appetite; it smelled like curry with rice. She was probably making lunch.

"This is so nostalgic…"

I stood in front of a wooden two-story dormitory. Only half a year had passed, but seeing it again was very moving.

I knocked on the door large enough for Ms. Paula to pass through, but no response came. *That's not surprising, I guess.* She tended to pour her whole heart into everything she did. She was probably so focused on cooking that she didn't hear me knock.

"Excuse me," I called out, and entered the dorm. I took off my shoes at the entrance, walked down the hall, and just as I thought, Ms. Paula was making lunch in the kitchen.

Paula Garedzall was the matron of the dorm I lived in while I was a student here. Standing at over 198 centimeters tall, she had a large build and a face with distinct features. She was wearing her usual outfit: a pure-white apron over a black shirt. Her sleeves were rolled up, baring arms that were three to five times bigger than mine.

That's weird… I've been training really hard. The difference in the size of our arms was even bigger than it was half a year ago. Her arms must have gotten even larger.

"Hmm-hmm-hmm…!"

She was stirring a pot cheerfully while humming in her unique, powerful manner. I cleared my throat and spoke up.

"Long time no see, Ms. Paula."

"…Hmm? Hey, if it isn't Allen! How are you…? Wait, what did you do with your hair?!" she asked, her large smile quickly disappearing as she stared at my head.

"I-is something wrong with my hair…?" I asked, confused.

"Wrong? Why, I've never seen anything like it! Here, look at yourself!" she said, giving me a hand mirror.

"Uh… what?!" I took the mirror and saw that my hair had turned a peculiar mix of black and white. "Wh-what happened?!" I shouted while running my hand through my transformed hair.

"What, you mean you didn't dye it?"

"I-I didn't!"

I think people call these "highlights"…? Regardless of what my new hairdo was called, it wasn't something I wanted.

"Did someone do it as a prank?" Ms. Paula asked.

"Umm… Maybe. I don't know," I answered.

Lia obviously wouldn't do this, and same for Rose. *That leaves the president… She had a mischievous streak, so it wasn't impossible. But when would she have had a chance to dye my hair?* I was sure I returned to the dorm after the celebration party. My memories were clear up to that point.

The problem is remembering what happened after that. There was an impenetrable gap in my memory from when I went to sleep that night to when I woke up in the forest. *That's really strange.*

Ms. Paula noticed my confused expression and clapped me on the back.

"Well, I admit it surprised me, but you can do whatever you want with your hair! I'm just happy to see you again! You look well!"

"…Thank you, Ms. Paula."

I was relieved to see her, too. She hadn't changed at all since I first met her.

"Oh yeah, I'll bet you haven't had lunch yet. Here, have some! It'll be just like old times!"

"Thanks, that would be great."

I washed my hands and rinsed my mouth in the bathroom and then sat down at the table.

"Dig in!" Ms. Paula said, before pouring curry onto a plate packed with rice.

"Ah-ha-ha… Your serving sizes are still enormous, I see…," I said, chuckling wryly. This was clearly enough food for five people.

"Hey, don't lose your nerve! You won't grow to be big and strong if you don't eat enough, okay?" she urged.

"I-I'll do my best…!"

I doubted I would ever get as big as Ms. Paula. Actually, I could say with confidence that I wouldn't. I wasn't sure if there was a single person in this world bigger than her.

"Thank you for the food."

"Sure thing. Enjoy!"

"I will!"

I dug my large spoon into the white rice and curry and ate a mouthful without hesitation. I tasted large potatoes, chewy beef cut into small bites, and liberally included hot spices. *This is Ms. Paula's cooking that I know and love!* I ate this food every day for three years, and it really hit the spot.

"How is it? Do you feel it giving you strength?" Ms. Paula asked.

"It's amazing!" I exclaimed.

"Ha-ha-ha, glad to hear it! Bring some friends next time!"

Rose didn't eat much, but Lia would probably lose her mind over this curry given how big a glutton she was. I continued to gulp down the curry and rice until an unsettling siren sounded from the radio.

"Hey, Allen, it's an emergency broadcast! That's unusual. I wonder what happened…?" she said. We both listened closely as a tense female broadcaster began to speak.

"Breaking news. Yesterday the Black Organization staged a large-scale assault on Thousand Blade Academy, located in the center of Aurest. There were no deaths, but many were injured. There is one missing student—a fifteen-year-old boy named Allen Rodol. The Holy Knights Association is currently conducting a far-reaching search, but he has not yet been found. If anyone has seen him—"

"…?! *Nggrh?!*" I was so shocked by the news that rice got caught in my throat and made me cough.

"Relax, Allen. Here, drink some water!" Ms. Paula advised.

"*Nng*… Phew… Th-thank you," I said after gulping down some water.

"No problem. Anyway, it sounds like something terrible happened. They said that you're missing. Is everything okay?"

"Y-yeah, everything's okay… I think…"

Fortunately, no one died. And if I was the only one missing, that meant Lia was okay. There was nothing to worry about at the moment.

I'm missing, though? What in the world…? Oh! Just then a tornado of information welled up from the depths of my brain.

"I-I remember now!"

That's right… I had fought the Black Organization that day. I broke their sturdy barrier using World Render and defeated Dodriel. Next I challenged Fuu Ludoras of the Thirteen Oracle Knights despite my exhaustion, and lost. Dodriel then recovered using a soul-crystal pill and stabbed me in the…heart… Huh?

He'd definitely stabbed me through the heart.

"…"

I quickly pulled up my shirt to look at my chest, but there was no scar. *What does this mean?* There was a major discrepancy between my memory and reality. *Did I just dream I was stabbed?* No, definitely not. I remembered the agonizing pain from being stabbed through the heart. There was no way that was a dream. Also, Thousand Blade was really attacked by the Black Organization.

If it actually happened, then why don't I even have a scar? Why did I wake up on the ground so far from Thousand Blade? *…It's no use. I can't make sense of it.* The only thing I could do was go to Thousand Blade and ask someone what happened directly.

"Ms. Paula, I…," I began.

"You're right, Allen. You should head back straight away and let everyone know you're okay," Ms. Paula agreed firmly before I even finished.

"Thank you, I will!"

I scarfed down the rest of the curry and rice.

"All right, bye, Ms. Paula!"

"Be careful out there!"

I dashed out of the dorm and began to run toward Thousand Blade. I felt something strange along the way. *My body feels so light…* I seemed to fly forward each time I kicked off the ground, almost as if I had grown wings. The scenery around me changed dramatically with each step. Before I knew it, I had arrived in Aurest.

That's weird. Was Aurest this close before…? I wondered in confusion as I walked through the city. My eyes went wide with shock when I reached Thousand Blade.

"What in the world?!"

Thousand Blade Academy was a mess of rubble. The main school building had been turned completely black, and a bottomless pit had been formed in the schoolyard. It was as if an inhuman monster had rampaged across the campus and destroyed everything in its wake.

BONUS CHAPTER
Allen Countermeasure Meeting

While Allen and Class 1-A were enjoying their celebration party after the Shadow Thousand Blade Festival, the core members of the Student Council were gathered in Shii's room in the House Arkstoria mansion.

"Okay... Let's start the Fifth Allen Countermeasure Meeting."

Student Council President Shii Arkstoria was running the meeting. She was wearing a lovely set of white pajamas, and had just gotten out of the bath. She plopped down onto her large bed and faced the other two attendees.

"Urgh... This is the fifth time we've held this secret meeting, and it hasn't gotten us anywhere yet...," complained Lilim.

"We always go so long, too... Is there even any point...?" grumbled Tirith.

Lilim was sitting cross-legged on a desk chair and Tirith was lazing on a sofa. They had made plans to sleep over at the Arkstoria mansion, so they were both wearing pajamas.

"Hey, I don't want to hear any whining!" Shii pouted, slapping her soft bed. She cleared her throat. "As you both know, we are facing a crisis of unprecedented proportions. If we don't find a way to knock Allen down a peg, the Student Council has no future!" she insisted, pointing at a framed picture on her desk.

Shii motioned emphatically to a framed picture on her desk. It was a picture of Allen Rodol performing a practice swing. She asked a servant of House Arkstoria to take the photo in secret the other day, and she was very fond of it.

"Wooow, that's a nice picture, Shii," Lilim said.

"You even have it framed…," Tirith observed.

They both grinned teasingly.

"Sh-shut up! We're not talking about that!" Shii yelled, blushing and pounding a fist on her bed. "A-anyway, our situation is grave. He beat us in the Club Budget War, he caught me cheating at poker, we let him down at the Sword Master Festival, he coasted through our haunted house, and to top it all off, he kicked our butts in the shadow festival. We've already lost all our cred as second years!"

"We've had one miserable failure after another…"

"We need to save face soon or there will be no recovery…"

Lilim's usual confidence appeared tarnished, and even the easygoing Tirith seemed to sense the danger they were in.

"We can't let a first year get the best of us any longer. That's why we're going to pull out all the stops in our next duel. We're going to challenge him three-on-one," Shii proposed.

"I-I don't know, that would feel kind of wrong…"

"There's no way that could be considered a fair fight…"

Lilim and Tirith both showed reluctance.

"We've used dirty methods already and still haven't managed to beat him once. Do you really think we could beat him fair and square at this rate?" Shii argued.

"W-well, you have a point… We wouldn't last two seconds if we challenged him one-on-one," Lilim admitted.

"My life just flashed before my eyes…," Tirith muttered.

Their faces went pale.

"We need to remember that we can't afford to lose focus, not even three-on-one. One moment of carelessness and we're done," Shii instructed.

"You're right. His speed is something else. He's got the strength of an ox packed into that slim body of his, too," Lilim responded.

"The darkness is the biggest problem of all. It strengthens him, defends him, and heals him all at the same time. It's so unfair…," Tirith grumbled.

They both recalled their defeat in the shadow festival and sighed loudly. Once the room started to turn gloomy, Shii clapped her hands.

"Okay, let's begin by analyzing his combat ability! I want to thoroughly discuss his strengths, weaknesses, habits, and more. We don't have time to wallow in misery!" she urged.

"Yeah… Let's do this!" Lilim agreed.

"Losing three-on-one would be beyond embarrassing. We have to make sure we win…!" Tirith said.

The Fifth Allen Countermeasure Meeting continued until dawn.

Afterword

Thank you very much for purchasing the fourth volume of *100-Million-Year Button*. I am the author, Syuichi Tsukishima.

I want to start by touching on the content of volume four. This will contain spoilers, so read on at your own risk.

This was another action-packed volume, featuring the Sword Master Festival, the Thousand Blade Festival, and the Black Organization assault. There were intense battles in each chapter, including Idora during the Sword Master Festival, the Student Council members during the Thousand Blade Festival, and Dodriel and Fuu during the Black Organization assault. I have a great love for battles, so writing them was a blast.

(By the way, the result of the Allen Countermeasure Meeting will be revealed in another original story…possibly.)

I will be very happy if this novel brings even a little joy to my readers. The fifth volume will feature a few very dense episodes, including the White Lily Girls Academy arc. It is scheduled for release in 2023, so please look forward to it!

Furthermore, the manga version of *100-Million-Year Button* is being published at Young Ace UP, and has been very well-received! The art really brings the story to life! The characters are expressive, the panels are clearly organized, and the pictures are dynamic! It could not have turned out better! I am taking part in the production as the original author, so please check it out.

Now, I would like to give some thanks.

To the illustrator Mokyu, the lead editor and the proofreader, and everyone else involved with the production of this book—thank you very much. And most of all, a huge thanks to all the readers who picked up volume four of *100-Million-Year Button*.

May we meet again when volume five releases Spring 2023.

Syuichi Tsukishima